CAUGHT IN THE MIDDLE

"I just can't go on like this, Sandy. I understand you're afraid to talk to your parents, but it isn't right. If you really loved me, you'd confront them," Manuel said.

Sandra's eyes filled with tears. "That isn't true. It's just that I need more time!"

"Yeah." A trace of bitterness crept into Manuel's voice. "That's what you've been saying for weeks, Sandy. I don't think you're being honest with yourself. I don't think you're ever going to be ready to confront them."

Sandra grabbed his arm, her eyes filled with panic. "Are you trying to tell me that you want to break up?"

"It isn't up to me," Manuel said sadly. "Sandy, I love you, but I need to feel that you respect me. Enough to confont your parents. Enough to tell everyone we're going out instead of hiding it!"

Sandra's eyes filled with tears. "Can't you give me just a little more ti............ed.

Manuel frow........................ I've been patient. ....with that he turned

SWEET VALLEY HIGH

CAUGHT IN THE MIDDLE

Written by
Kate William

Created by
FRANCINE PASCAL

BANTAM BOOKS
TORONTO • NEW YORK • LONDON • SYDNEY • AUCKLAND

RL 6, IL age 12 and up

CAUGHT IN THE MIDDLE

A Bantam Book / January 1988

Sweet Valley High is a registered trademark of Francine Pascal.

Conceived by Francine Pascal.

Produced by Cloverdale Press, Inc.
135 Fifth Avenue, New York, NY 10003

Cover art by James Mathewuse

ISBN 0-553-26951-8

Published simultaneously in the United States and Canada

Bantam Books are published by Bantam Books, Inc. Its trademark, consisting of the words "Bantam Books" and the portrayal of a rooster, is Registered in U.S. Patent and Trademark Office and in other countries. Marca Registrada. Bantam Books, Inc., 666 Fifth Avenue, New York, New York 10103.

PRINTED IN THE UNITED STATES OF AMERICA

O   0 9 8 7 6 5 4 3 2 1

CAUGHT IN THE MIDDLE

One

"I still can't believe it," Jessica Wakefield said to Cara Walker as the two girls walked toward one of the sunlit fields of the Sweet Valley High grounds for cheerleading practice. "Who on earth would've believed that Sandy and Manuel would fall in love."

"I don't see what's so strange about it," Cara protested. "Actually, I think they make a good couple." She smiled. "And it explains why Sandy's looking so different lately, so radiant. I should've guessed she was madly in love!"

Jessica frowned and leaned down to straighten a white ankle sock. "Cara, you've really changed," she said critically as she stood up again. Before Cara started dating Steven, Jessica's older brother, she and Jessica had been best friends, sharing opinions on everything that mattered. But for ages now Cara had been getting "soft," as Jessica put it, and that meant she hadn't been filling her in on the latest gossip. This seemed like a typical case. Cara had apparently known for a couple of days that Sandra Bacon was seeing Manuel Lopez, and she hadn't even confided in Jessica! If they hadn't spotted the couple embracing in a deserted corridor a few moments earlier, Jessica might *never* have found out about Sweet Valley High's newest couple. She frowned at the thought. Jessica prided herself on always being up on the latest in everything, from fashions to music to gossip. And she hated to think Cara might have deliberately excluded her from something as important as Sandra's brand-new romance with Manuel. Even worse was the sentimental look on Cara's face as she contemplated their romance. Not that Jessica wasn't completely in favor of romance. It was just that lately most of her friends seemed to be getting involved in long-term, heavy-duty relationships. Her twin sister, Elizabeth, was one of the offenders. You couldn't get her to go *anywhere* without Jeffrey French. "Boyfriends," Jessica grumbled. "I think people would be better off playing the field."

Cara laughed and tossed back her dark brown, shoulder-length hair. "Like you, right?" she teased. "Look, Jess, just because *you* go through

2

guys faster than any of us can keep up with, doesn't mean we *all* have to! Besides," she added with a significant smile, "there's nothing like *real* love."

Jessica rolled her eyes. "Yeah, I'll bet. Instead of having the fun of going out with a new guy every weekend, you're always stuck with the same one. And soon all the fun disappears. No more presents or surprise phone calls, no more expensive dates. He figures he's got you just where he wants you and whammo!—no more romance. He starts taking you for granted, and you start doing things like Jeffrey and Liz—*studying* together and boring things like that." Jessica grimaced.

Cara laughed out loud as the two approached the bleachers where the cheerleaders were gathering for afternoon practice. "That's the most negative description of love I've heard from you in a while. Sounds to me like you're about due for one of those incredible Jessica Wakefield-style crushes, the kind that make you forget all your theories and just really flip."

Jessica smiled. "Maybe you're right. It *has* been a while," she admitted.

"Jessica! Cara! What's taking you so long?" Ricky Capaldo demanded, waving them over. Ricky, a short, energetic junior with a strong sense of organization, was the cheerleaders' manager. Once he had dated one of the cheerlead-

3

ers, pretty, dark-haired Annie Whitman. Now he joked that just making sure they all got to practice—and actually worked through their routines—left him no time for anything else. Jessica and Robin Wilson were co-captains of the team, and the other members included Cara; Annie; Sandra Bacon; her best friend Jeanie West; a petite brunette named Maria Santelli; and Amy Sutton, one of Jessica's closest friends. They were all there now, except for Sandra.

"Let's get started!" Ricky exclaimed. "We can't wait any longer, or we're never going to get through this. We'll just have to explain it to Sandy when she shows up. And remember," he added, "we want to save time at the end of practice to talk about that cheerleading competition to raise money for the Regina Morrow Scholarship Fund." Everyone grew serious at the mention of the special fund, started by Pi Beta Alpha, the sorority of which Jessica was president. The fund had been set up in memory of the junior who had died recently of an extremely rare reaction to a small amount of cocaine. A scholarship would be awarded to a student at Sweet Valley High who overcame a handicap or hardship, and the cheerleaders, Jessica in particular, were eager to raise money for the fund.

Ricky cleared his throat. "Robin, do you want

to run through that new kick once to show the group, before we all try it together?"

Jeanie looked perturbed. "I wish Sandy would hurry up," she said in a low voice. "She knows practice starts earlier on Tuesday afternoons!"

"She's with Manuel," Maria whispered. "I saw them in the hall after the last-period bell."

Jessica listened intently. Jeanie was Sandra's closest friend, and Jessica wondered what she thought of her friend's new romance. After all, Manuel came from a completely different world. His family was from Mexico and still spoke Spanish at home. Manuel had always hung around with the Mexican kids at school. Sandra's parents had a reputation for being strict with their only daughter, who was also the youngest in her family. Moreover, they were reputed to be bigoted. Lila Fowler, one of Jessica's best friends, claimed that Mr. Bacon had written a letter to the local paper complaining about minority members and immigrants ruining the community. Jessica wondered how they were reacting to Manuel as their daughter's boyfriend.

Before Jeanie had a chance to respond to Maria, Sandra herself came dashing up, her face pink and her breathing ragged from running across the field. "Sorry I'm late," she gasped, falling into place beside Jeanie. Her hazel eyes were bright and her short, dark blond hair—usually very neat—was a mess. Jessica was surprised at how pretty she looked. Not that she wasn't cute, but being best friends with Jeanie, one of the acclaimed beauties of the school, she was always complaining about looking "just average."

And Jessica had secretly been inclined to agree. She knew Sandra fairly well, both through cheerleading and through Pi Beta Alpha, which Sandra had belonged to for some time. She was the sort of girl Jessica never really paid that much attention to, though. Cute enough, nice enough, smart enough, but to Jessica there was nothing really striking about her.

But Jessica had to admit that Sandra looked different that afternoon. Her eyes sparkled, and her smile was radiant.

Maybe Cara was right, Jessica thought grudgingly as she took her place at the front of the squad beside Robin. Maybe Sandra really *was* changing now that she had fallen in love with Manuel Lopez.

"Hey, Sandy," Jeanie said, twisting her long hair into a single braid. "Tell me what's up with you and Manuel. I was getting worried about you this afternoon. I thought you were going to miss practice."

Jeanie and Sandra were in the locker room changing after practice and after the scholarship fund discussion. The others had all dressed and gone already, and the two girls had the whole place to themselves.

Sandra gave her friend a rapturous smile. "Jeanie, he's unbelievable! I've never met a guy who's like Manuel before. He's smart, and thoughtful, and funny, and sweet, and—"

"Whoa!" Jeanie laughed, putting up her hand. "Back up a minute before you give me the list of virtues. What's the story with you two? Are you actually going out or still just friends? I've never known you to keep anything important so secret before."

Sandra looked down at the floor. "I know," she admitted. "I wish. . ." Her expression darkened for a minute, then cleared again. "Look, Jeanie, I want to tell you everything. But you have to promise me you won't repeat any of it, OK? I just feel—you know—kind of shy about the whole thing. I don't want anyone to know but you."

"All right, so tell me." Jeanie smiled, then sat down on a bench and looked at her friend expectantly.

"Well," Sandra began, giggling a little at her own awkwardness, "I guess it's official now. We're going out. He's taking me over to his cousin's house for a party on Friday night. I'll get to meet his whole family there." She smiled. "I know they must be wonderful. The way Manuel talks about his parents and brothers you can just tell." She sighed. "I think that's one of the things I like so much about him. He comes from a big family, and they're all very close. I think that's why he's so affectionate, always holding my hand or putting his arm around me." She blushed. "I think he really likes me, Jeanie, really thinks I'm special."

Jeanie laughed, then jumped up to give her friend a hug. "He'd better! Because you *are* special," she declared.

Sandra's eyes shone. "You're the most wonderful friend," she said in a shaky voice. "Jeanie, I don't know what I'd do without you."

Neither girl spoke for a minute. Sandra was remembering, with a pang, how close she had come to spoiling their friendship several months back when Jeanie pledged Pi Beta Alpha. It had been a particularly hard time for Sandra then. She was feeling extremely vulnerable and insecure, and she had become convinced that she was really nothing but Jeanie's shadow. Jeanie did everything so perfectly and was so stunning. Sandra had become convinced that Jeanie would tire of their friendship unless she did something to even things out between them. Sandra had also convinced herself that once Jeanie was admitted to the sorority, she wouldn't need her anymore and their friendship would fall apart. It made Sandra cringe now to think how idiotically she had behaved. She had purposely tried to sabotage her own best friend! When Jeanie found out that Sandra was trying to exclude her from the sorority, she had been rightly enraged. Fortunately, Sandra was able to see what a fool she'd been before it was too late, and the two had made up. Now Jeanie was a member of Pi Beta Alpha, and—as she had assured Sandra from the start—it just gave them more chances to see each other. They were better friends than ever.

"Well," Jeanie said lightly, patting Sandra's arm, "I guess I'm not going to be seeing much of you now that you're in love. Are you going to bring Manuel to the picnic my parents are having this weekend?"

The Wests and the Bacons were good friends and had arranged a get-together that weekend at Secca Lake. But Sandra had no intention of bringing Manuel, and her expression revealed how upset it made her to imagine what would happen if she did. "Jeanie," she said, distressed, "promise not to mention Manuel to my parents, will you?"

Jeanie was surprised. "Why? Haven't they met him yet? I thought you said you two were official."

"Well, we are," Sandra said. "But no, they haven't met him yet. And I don't think they're going to, either. At least, not for a while."

"Why not? That's crazy," Jeanie objected.

"Oh, yeah? Aren't you forgetting the way my parents feel about Mexicans? I wish they weren't as bigoted as they are, but I've got to face facts. What would be crazy would be showing up with my arm through Manuel's and saying he was my boyfriend." Sandra shook her head. "My dad would have a heart attack. And my mom would ground me on the spot."

Jeanie frowned. "That's too bad. I know your parents aren't as open-minded as they could be, but . . ."

"Yeah." Sandra sighed. "Sad to say, but true. And it isn't just a superficial prejudice with them. I know how they really feel, and they'd kill me, absolutely kill me, if they knew about Manuel." She shook her head. "No, I just can't tell them yet. I'm going to have to break it to them gradually."

"Well," Jeanie said as she took her jacket out of her locker, "your secret's safe with me. But I don't really see how you plan on having a relationship with Manuel without them finding out."

10

Sandra didn't answer. Jeanie just didn't understand. There was no way they could find out! If they did, that would be the end of her and Manuel.

And she wasn't going to let that happen. Not now, not when she had finally found the perfect boy.

"Jessica," Elizabeth said, putting a cold, wet hand on her twin sister's shoulder, "I hate to interrupt your beauty sleep, but isn't it your turn to make dinner tonight?"

Jessica groaned. She and Lila Fowler had spread towels out near the Wakefields' swimming pool in the backyard, and Jessica had dozed off in the middle of one of Lila's stories about her latest crush. Jessica was right in the middle of a wonderful dream in which Lila had decided she was sick of being the richest girl at Sweet Valley High and was writing a check to Jessica giving her all her money, when Elizabeth woke her up.

"Can't you see we're sleeping?" Jessica grumbled, sitting up with an effort. Lila, still lying down, emitted a long groan. "Go 'way," she mumbled sleepily.

"You two are pathetic," Elizabeth said, crossing her arms. "I thought cheerleading gave you

11

lots of energy, Jess. You look like a limp rag to me."

Jessica eyed her sister silently, then turned to Lila. "How is it possible," Jessica asked, "that this efficient, organized taskmaster can be related to me?"

"Good question," Lila mumbled. "I think you split the beauty, and she got the brains, Jess."

Jessica took a swipe at her friend. "Come on inside and help me make dinner," she begged.

"Make dinner?" Lila said blankly.

"Yeah, it's what the rest of the world does while your cook makes yours." Jessica giggled. Lila Fowler was the only child of one of the richest men in the state. Fowler Crest, the mansion in which she lived, resembled a Hollywood movie set, and the Fowlers had several servants. Jessica eyed Lila thoughtfully as they got to their feet and folded up their towels. "You know, I bet you'd find it pretty interesting to trade places with me for a while," she said slowly, thinking about her dream. "You could live here with Elizabeth and my parents. And I—"

"Forget it," Lila said. "Your house is fun to visit, but I need closet space, Jess. Daddy's bringing me back a bunch of new clothes from Rome for my birthday."

Jessica groaned. She and Lila followed Elizabeth into the Wakefields' cheerful, Spanish-style kitchen, and Jessica took the hamburger meat out of the refrigerator, then looked helplessly around for a bowl.

"Here it is," Elizabeth said with a sigh, handing her a bowl. "Why is it that I can tell I'm going to end up making dinner again tonight?"

Jessica gave her a hurt look. "I'm making it," she protested. "I'm just moving a little slowly, that's all. Come on, Liz, give me a break."

"Oh, wow. Is it time for 'The Jessica and Elizabeth Show' already?" Lila teased them.

They all laughed, and Jessica set to work making the hamburgers. It was true. On the outside she and Elizabeth were like photocopies of each other. Five-foot-six, with long, sun-streaked blond hair and sparkling blue-green eyes, they looked exactly alike, down to the tiny dimple each girl had in her left cheek. Only the tiny mole on Elizabeth's right shoulder set her apart. But Elizabeth, who was four minutes older than her twin, was as earnest, responsible, and even-tempered as Jessica was impetuous and headstrong. Jessica did everything by whim, whereas Elizabeth loved to sit down and plan. The extreme disparity in their personalities was reflected in their hobbies, their friends, and even the way they decorated their rooms. Elizabeth spent most of her spare time working for *The Oracle*, the school paper. She wanted to be a writer one day and took the paper very seriously. Her best friend, Enid Rollins, liked the same sort of things she did—listening to music, taking long walks, reading. And her boyfriend, Jeffrey French, shared her interests as well. Jeffrey was a photographer for *The Oracle*, and they both loved movies, long talks—and each other!

Jessica got bored even imagining her sister's idea of fun. In her heart she loved Elizabeth more than anyone in the world, and the two had a special bond that she valued enormously. But Jessica liked to tease her twin, claiming she was too steady, too dependable. And Elizabeth liked to reproach Jessica, claiming she was irresponsible. It *did* make for showdowns from time to time, and Jessica knew what Lila meant by ''The Jessica and Elizabeth Show.'' But she couldn't resist getting back at her friend with a sharp comment of her own.

''Better than 'Life-styles of the Rich and Famous','' she muttered, adding some spices to the hamburger meat.

Lila ignored this jab. ''You know,'' she announced, ''my birthday happens to be a week from this Saturday.''

Jessica and Elizabeth exchanged glances. "Really?" Jessica said, winking at her twin.

"And I was thinking how great it would be if, you know, maybe someone had a party for me. I mean, I've had so many parties for my friends. . . ." She let her words trail off meaningfully.

"That *would* be nice," Jessica said noncommittally. "I hope someone does that for you, Li."

Lila looked furious. "I have to go home now," she snapped, grabbing her things.

Jessica pretended not to notice how irate her friend was. "OK, see you tomorrow!" she called cheerfully, as Lila stomped off toward the front hall.

"That wasn't very nice, Jess," Elizabeth said. "She was obviously hoping you'd volunteer to have a surprise party for her here."

"Yeah, I know," Jessica said blithely. "But that wouldn't be much of a surprise, would it?" She giggled. "Typical Lila. She's so used to bossing around her servants that she doesn't know what to do when someone doesn't do exactly what she wants."

"Well," Elizabeth said, "you weren't very nice about it."

"I thought you hated Lila," Jessica reminded her.

Elizabeth thought this over. It was true that there was no love lost between Lila Fowler and her. Elizabeth found the girl spoiled and haughty, and she had often said to Jessica that Lila was a snob. "I'm not her biggest fan. But she *does* have a point, Jess. She must have about one party a month at her place. And a lot of them have been for other people."

"Well, I happen to have been planning a party for her," Jessica said loftily. "But it's going to be a *real* surprise. Which means that it isn't going to be on Saturday night, as she thinks it will."

"Oh? When is it going to be?"

"Sunday night, the day after her birthday," Jessica said happily, making hamburger patties with her usual lack of care. "And the best thing is, I'm going to tell everyone to act like they couldn't care less about her birthday. She'll be so mad! I bet she'll stop talking to all of us," she concluded happily.

Elizabeth shook her head. "Some friend," she remarked. "I'm glad you're not throwing a party for me."

"Well, you're invited," Jessica reminded her. "Just make sure not to let Lila know that you've even given her birthday the tiniest little bit of thought."

As Elizabeth opened the refrigerator, she said cheerfully, "You know, Jessica, I have a feeling I won't have much trouble giving Lila that impression!"

"Good," Jessica said, ignoring her sister's veiled sarcasm.

There was nothing Jessica loved better than a scheme. And something told her this was a party she was really going to enjoy planning!

Two

"Promise you'll call me tonight," Manuel said huskily in his slightly accented voice, cupping Sandra's chin in his hand. He had been waiting for her when she and Jeanie got out of practice and had insisted on driving her home, even though she would have been happy to walk. Sandra felt she had to pinch herself to prove she wasn't coming. Manuel was so unlike any other guy she had known. He was a junior as she was, but he acted years older and even *looked* slightly older. Sandra loved his dark, curly hair and chocolate-brown eyes. Manuel was on the track team and had a terrific build, too. He wasn't terribly tall, but then neither was she, and it was nice to be able to look up just a little bit to stare into his eyes. Being with him made her tingle all over.

And the way he treated her! *That* was the best part. No one had ever been so good to her before. But then, she had never been in love before either, never even had a serious crush. She always had had a number of male friends, but her philosophy had always been to remain friends with them. Perhaps it was because she had three older brothers, or perhaps it was because of the pattern she saw so many girls fall into—waiting around for some guy to call or getting upset over a boyfriend who didn't really reciprocate the affection.

But Manuel was different. Everything about him was soft and sincere. He had a low, sexy voice that trembled when he said her name. And he was incredibly dedicated. When he joined a club or a sport, he threw himself into it wholeheartedly. As he had explained to Sandra the first time they had had a real conversation a few weeks ago, when she was cheering at a track meet, he probably acted older than his age because he had so many younger siblings to take care of—four brothers and one sister. Manuel was used to responsibility, and it showed. He had a part-time job coaching track at the elementary school, and he clearly enjoyed it. When Sandra had asked him if he needed to work, he looked at her thoughtfully. "I'm saving up to help pay for college," he said. "My dad makes a good living, but with six kids we're all going to have to help out. I'm the oldest, and I want to set a good example."

That, Sandra thought as she let herself in the front door of the Spanish-style house her parents had had built ten years ago, was another of the things she admired about Manuel. He knew exactly what he wanted, and he wouldn't let anything get in his way.

Thinking of the expression on his face just now when they had said goodbye made her stomach do flip-flops. It was kind of dizzying, the way she was falling for him, and she knew he felt the same way. It was all happening so fast! Three weeks ago she had barely known who he was. Now, even a few hours at school without seeing him seemed like agony. And just picturing his dark, handsome face made her shiver. If this was what love was like, no wonder everyone made such a big deal out of it!

"Sandy? Is that you?" Mrs. Bacon asked, coming out of the kitchen and wiping her hands on a towel. "I'm just finishing up a cake for dessert tonight. Why don't you come keep me company and tell me how your day was?"

Sandra took her jacket off and followed her mother somewhat reluctantly into the kitchen. This was a ritual she ordinarily loved—sitting

20

on one of the high wooden stools in the kitchen and chatting with her mother about everything from current events to homework to gossip at school. None of her brothers lived at home anymore, and Sandy knew it made her mother happy to still have her around. As the baby of the family, she had always been showered with affection and attention from both of her parents, especially her mother. In the past, she had confided in her mother about *everything*. But now she wondered if she didn't tell her mother *too* much about her personal life—and if her mother didn't pry too much. *I'm only thinking this because of Manuel,* she reminded herself uneasily. *Before Manuel I didn't have anything to hide from Mom and Dad. But now I do.*

"Hey, look at this!" Sandy exclaimed, picking up the community newspaper from the counter as she sat on the stool. "I didn't know there was going to be a Mexican festival in Sweet Valley! This looks wonderful." She pointed to the cover story on the front page of the paper. It described the festival, which would take place in a couple of weeks. Mrs. Bacon frowned as she spread icing on the cake she had baked.

"I have to admit I've got some misgivings," she said. "Don't you remember what happened during that festival in Los Perros, when those riots broke out and people got hurt?" She shook

21

her head. "It may sound terrible, but I wish they'd cancel the festival. I don't like the idea."

Sandra stared at her mother. "Why?" she cried. "Mom, what can possibly go wrong? You just think Mexicans are hot-tempered, that they start riots," she added, horrified by her mother's unconcealed prejudice.

Mrs. Bacon shrugged. "I don't know what I think. I just know that we've seen enough racial tension in this part of the state to last for a long time." Her eyes were dark with concern. "Remember," she added, "I grew up in a neighborhood where racial violence tore the community apart. I know what it's like." Mrs. Bacon had grown up in a town plagued with racial tension, and it had left permanent marks on her. But this time Sandra did not feel sympathetic.

She felt her face burn with anger. "Well, canceling the festival doesn't sound like the answer to me, Mom," she said, trying to sound calm. "The Mexicans in Sweet Valley should be proud of their heritage. I think this festival sounds great."

"As long as you stay far away from it," Mrs. Bacon said, unaware of the effect her words had on her daughter, "I guess I think it's fine, too." She smiled lovingly at her daughter. "You've always been open-minded, Sandy. And

I'm proud of you for that. Just make sure you don't blind yourself. You know what kind of trouble those people can cause."

Sandra felt tears welling up in her eyes. *Those people!* How could her mother say something like that? It made her sick to her stomach. "I don't know what you mean," she choked out with difficulty. "How are 'those people' any different from us, Mom?"

"Sandy," Mrs. Bacon said reproachfully. "They're completely different! Why do you think they're having this festival? They want to remind themselves of all the customs they have that keep them separate from the rest of us. They have a different language and different customs. They're foreigners, not Americans."

Sandra climbed down from the stool. Her head was throbbing, and the warm feeling she'd had when she first got home was gone. What an idiot she had been to think she could gradually reconcile her parents to the idea of her and Manuel. She was right. They would kill her if they found out!

She looked at her mother with uncertainty. For the first time she could remember, she found herself in complete disagreement with her mother. "They *are* Americans, Mom," she said weakly.

Mrs. Bacon raised her eyebrows in surprise. "Why, Sandy," she said. "It isn't like you to be so stubborn. Remember, your father and I have lived in this community a lot longer than you have. It's nice to be idealistic, but you're still very young, honey. I'm afraid you haven't seen enough of the world yet to judge."

Sandra wet her lips nervously. She wished she had the courage to talk back to her mother. But she had never disagreed with her about anything before. It made her feel awful to realize how far apart they were on this.

One thing was certain. She was going to have to do everything she could to make sure they didn't find out about Manuel.

"Sandy," Mr. Bacon said at dinner, giving her an affectionate smile, "I think I may have found a nice young man for you. Someone just perfect for that spring dance coming up at the country club."

Sandra pushed the food around on her plate, her appetite gone. "Oh, really?" she said, turning bright red. She had forgotten all about the dance. In truth, Sandra wasn't all that fond of the events the club organized for young people. She thought they were pretty stuffy. But her parents were serious golfers and liked the club a lot, and they always seemed hurt if Sandra didn't join them for special family events.

"Remember I told you a new man had joined our team on the Brice campaign?" Mr. Bacon said to his wife. Mr. Bacon worked at a local advertising agency. "Well, he has a son who sounds perfect for Sandy! His name is Carl Pierce. He's a senior at Westwood High. And he plays golf," he added triumphantly, as if that clinched it.

Sandra cut her chicken into smaller pieces, convinced she would die if she put even one tiny shred into her mouth. All she had to do was close her eyes, and she could picture Carl Pierce. He probably had blond hair and blue eyes and looked exactly like every other guy at the club. The thought of going to the spring dance with him and talking about *golf* made her wince.

"Sandy? Aren't you interested in meeting a nice boy?" Mrs. Bacon asked.

Sandra looked helplessly from one parent to the other. For the first time she could remember, her parents' love and attention felt oppressive to her. Why couldn't they leave her alone, let her make some of her own choices?

"Will you excuse me?" she said, getting to her feet. "I'm tired out from practice. I don't feel very well."

"But you haven't even touched your food!

And I made that special cake for dessert," Mrs. Bacon cried.

"Irene, leave her alone," Mr. Bacon admonished. Sandra didn't hear him. She was already out of the room. She could hardly wait to call Manuel.

"Cara? It's me, Jessica," Jessica announced into the phone. She was curled up in the chair in her bedroom, a list of names on a piece of paper in her hand. She had already told Amy Sutton all about the "surprise" surprise party for Lila, and Amy thought it was as great an idea as she did. Amy had volunteered to call half the names on Jessica's list, and Jessica had given her careful instructions to tell everyone to act as if they didn't know Lila's birthday was coming up. Whenever Lila mentioned it, they were just supposed to ignore her. And some kind of event would have to be scheduled for Saturday, Lila's actual birthday, so everyone could say they were going to it, underscoring how little Lila's birthday mattered.

"I don't know," Cara said dubiously when Jessica had filled her in on the plan. "Isn't that kind of—I don't know—kind of *mean*?"

"Cara!" Jessica shrieked. "This is *Lila*, remember? The girl whose father is bringing her back the entire inventory from every boutique in Rome? The one who wears designer underwear?"

"Still," Cara protested weakly, "I don't know, Jess."

"The one," Jessica added, gathering steam, "who told you she thought your spring wardrobe was two years out of date?"

"You have a point," Cara said. "And anyway, I guess the end result will be nice. I mean, we *will* give her a surprise party after all."

"Right!" Jessica exclaimed. "Now remember, Cara. Not a *word* about her birthday. And if Lila drags it into the conversation, just yawn and change the subject."

Cara giggled. "You're terrible," she said.

Jessica grinned. She just couldn't wait to see the look on Lila's face when she thought that no one cared about her birthday.

Three

"Carlos!" Manuel scolded his younger brother, picking up the squirming six-year-old in his arms. "Don't you realize that Sandy may not consider it fun when you roll your toy trucks all over her. She's not a road, she's a person!"

Carlos's face fell, and Sandra laughed. "He's not bothering me," she protested. It was Thursday afternoon, and she and Manuel were at his house, keeping an eye on his little brothers. Manuel's mother had gone out to the store, and Sandra and Manuel were trying to think of inventive ways to keep four little boys from killing one another. Sandra thought the little Lopez boys were wonderful. Carlos was the youngest; then came Juan, Pedro, and Miguel. Maria, the only girl, was thirteen. She was watching Sandra shyly from across the crowded living room.

28

"Boy," Sandra said, smiling, "I can imagine how Maria feels. It's tough having so many brothers. I have three myself, but they're much older than I am."

"Well, my brothers are a lot of work," Maria said, giggling. "You should see what it's like doing laundry around this place." She rumpled Pedro's hair. "And they *eat* so much!"

"But a big family is a lot of fun," Manuel said thoughtfully. "Has it been lonesome for you since your brothers left home?"

Sandra thought that over. She had lived alone with her parents for the past four years. She was pretty used to it by now. "Not really. My parents and I are really close," she said. *Except lately*, she added to herself. Lately, it *was* lonesome at home, because she was keeping something so important a secret.

Bringing up her parents just then wasn't the best idea. A shadow crossed Manuel's face. "Well, I'm looking forward to meeting them," he said, giving her hand a squeeze. Manuel had already asked about her parents several times, explaining that he felt uncomfortable dating her without having met them. And she hadn't the heart yet to explain that her parents were going to be a problem. She'd just invented excuses, saying they were really busy lately. She felt so guilty about lying to him, too. But she hated to think how much it would hurt him if he knew the truth—that her parents were prejudiced.

Glancing around the Lopezes' cheerful, cluttered living room, Sandra couldn't help thinking how different it looked from her own house. The Lopez household seemed so much more casual. Even when her brothers had been at home, thought Sandra, her mother had insisted on order. In the Lopez living room there were games and toys everywhere, the television set was turned on, and everyone was chattering and laughing. It was more like a party than a family gathering. When Mrs. Lopez came back from the store, real chaos erupted. All the little boys wanted to help her unload groceries. Everyone went into the kitchen, and the boys kept getting in one another's way.

"Sandy, you're staying for dinner," Mrs. Lopez declared, taking a package of ground beef out of a shopping bag. "We're having homemade tortillas tonight. Stay, and Maria and I will show you how to make them."

Sandra deliberated. She'd have to think of something to tell her parents. "I don't know," she said. "It's sweet of you to offer, but—"

"No buts!" Mrs. Lopez cried with mock severity. "Please stay," she said, her expression warm. "We really would love to have you."

Sandra blushed a little under her direct gaze.

It made her feel terrible, imagining how *her* mother would treat Manuel under similar circumstances. She had never seen her own family in a negative light before, and it hurt her to realize how much they suffered in comparison.

"I'd like to stay, but I should call my parents," she faltered.

"Call them!" Mrs. Lopez exclaimed, making little motions toward the phone. "Tell them we're teaching you how real Mexicans cook!"

Sandra's blush deepened as she looked at the phone. Something told her that wasn't exactly the right tactic. "Could I—would you mind if I used the phone in the living room?" she asked, even more embarrassed.

"Go right ahead," Mrs Lopez said. "It will certainly be quieter!" She gave two of her little boys affectionate shoves as they once again managed to get in her way. "Out of the way, you two," she scolded. "Can't you see I'm trying to unload the groceries?"

"I'll be back in a minute," Sandra said to Manuel. She walked into the living room and sat down on the couch by the phone. *That was close*, she thought. She could hardly lie to her mother right there on the kitchen phone in front of everyone!

She dialed her number quickly and waited for her mother to say hello. "Mom, it's Sandy," she said, trying to sound casual. "I'm over at Jeanie's. Can I stay here for dinner?"

"Are you sure Mrs. West doesn't mind?" her mother asked. "You've been going over there a lot lately."

Sandra fidgeted. "She doesn't mind."

"Well, all right. Don't stay too late, dear. I'll see you later," her mother said.

Sandra replaced the receiver.

"Hey," Manuel said, staring at her from the doorway. She hadn't heard him walk down the hallway. "What's going on? Why'd you tell your mom you're over at Jeanie's?"

She stared at him, tongue-tied. "I—uh, I—"

Manuel's face colored. "I get it," he said, his voice terse and unhappy. "You don't want them to know about me, do you? All that stuff about introducing me to them was just meant to put me off until you told me the truth."

"Manuel," Sandra said with difficulty, "my parents are very old-fashioned, very narrow-minded. Some of their ideas . . ."

Manuel seemed so hurt that Sandra thought she might burst out crying.

"I'm going to tell them about you," she said quickly. "It's just that I think they need a little time, that's all."

"I don't see what time has to do with it,"

Manuel said quietly. "What's the problem? You think they'll object to me because I'm Mexican?"

Sandra stared down at the floor. It sounded so horrible when he put it like that, so disgusting. Shame for her parents flooded over her. "They—they can't help it. They don't mean to be like they are. I mean basically they're good people. It's just—"

"Sure," Manuel said, his voice bitter. "I know. All my life I've met people like that, basically good people, who think just because my last name is Lopez and my skin is brown instead of white, that I'm not worth bothering with." His eyes filled with sadness. "I'm just sorry your parents are like that, that's all. But I'm not surprised. I guess in a community like this one, you get used to prejudice, and you learn to live with it."

Sandra crossed the room and put her arms around him, her eyes filling with tears. "Manuel," she murmured, "I'd do anything to make them change their minds! I can't stand sneaking around behind their backs. It makes me feel terrible."

Manuel was quiet for a minute. "Would you really do anything?" he asked her. "Then why not talk to them? Let them meet me?"

Sandra didn't answer. "Soon," she said at

last, her voice muffled against his chest. "Just give me a little time."

"Hi!" Mrs. Bacon called from the living room when Sandra opened the front door at eight-thirty. "How was dinner at Jeanie's? Did her parents talk about the barbecue?"

Sandra bit her lip as she took off her jacket. She had forgotten they were all getting together that weekend. Now her mother was bound to say something to the Wests about having her over so often. She made a mental note to call Jeanie as soon as she got to her room and warn her she'd been using her as a cover. "It was nice," she said, avoiding the question of the barbecue.

After hanging her jacket up in the front hall closet, she wandered into the living room. Her mother was knitting and watching TV, and her father was sitting at the desk doing some paperwork. Again, Sandra thought of the contrast between this rather formal room and the comfortable clutter at the Lopezes' house. She sat down on the couch beside her mother. "That's pretty," she said automatically, touching the soft, blue yarn.

"It's for you," her mother said, smiling at her. "How's Jeanie? Is she still spending a lot of time with Tom?"

Sandra nodded. "Mom," she said, picking up

34

her mother's yarn and pulling thoughtfully at one strand, "you know how you and Dad are always saying you'd like me to meet a nice boy. Someone like Carl Pierce, who Dad wanted to fix me up with." She cleared her throat. "What if I told you that I'd met someone really nice— but he was from a different background. Say, a Mexican-American, for example."

"Good heavens," Mrs. Bacon said, frowning at Sandra. "I certainly hope this is a hypothetical situation, Sandy. I also hope you know your father and me well enough to realize that the last thing on earth we want for you is to get involved with just anybody." From the tone of her voice, "just anybody" clearly meant someone undesirable. Someone Mexican.

Sandra got to her feet, her heart heavy. It was just as bad as she had thought it would be. "But why?" she managed to choke out. "If he was really nice and everything, and had all the qualities you value most."

Mrs. Bacon looked seriously at her. "Because I'd be afraid you'd get hurt in the long run. They're different from us, Sandy. It took me most of my childhood and adolescence to find that out. But once I did. . . ." Mrs. Bacon's expression was sad. Sandra could tell the discussion was over.

How was she supposed to confront her parents? They were set in their ways. And she herself had never rebeled about anything. All her life she had been obedient, and she knew it would hurt them if she disagreed with something they cared about so deeply. And she had always felt so responsible for not hurting them, because she was the only girl and her parents were older than most of her friends' parents.

"Don't worry. I was talking off the top of my head," Sandra said. "I'm going to go upstairs now."

She could tell from the expression on her mother's face that she was disappointing her. Mrs. Bacon wanted her to stay downstairs and tell them all about her day. But Sandra didn't feel like being with them just then. Her parents suddenly were a disappointment to *her*.

But her real disappointment was in herself. She simply didn't have the courage to tell her parents the truth.

"So anyway," Sandra concluded breathlessly into the telephone, "will you help me out this weekend when my folks start grilling you about me coming over for dinner and that sort of stuff?"

"OK, San," Jeanie said doubtfully. "I hope you can carry it off. I know how strict your parents are. But if they start suspecting that something's up—"

"They won't!" Sandra said defensively. "How can they possibly find out if I don't tell them?"

"Well, word is getting out about you and Manuel. In fact, I meant to tell you, a couple of the girls were talking today at the Pi Beta meeting, and somehow it came out that you and Manuel are going to be mentioned in the 'Eyes and Ears' column in *The Oracle* next week. Amy Sutton is the one who told me." Amy was known to say whatever was on her mind with little or no regard for other people's feelings.

Sandra's stomach did a flip-flop. *The Oracle*, the student paper at Sweet Valley High, was exactly where she did *not* want her private life mentioned. Especially since Mrs. Bacon often asked to read the paper, just to keep up on school life.

"Jeanie," she said desperately, "if my mom sees that—"

"Well, maybe you should find Liz Wakefield tomorrow at school and tell her not to write about you in the column," Jeanie said. "Anyway, all I'm saying is that people are starting to notice the two of you. And you know how it is in a place as small as Sweet Valley—it's practically impossible to keep anything a secret."

Sandra's mouth was dry. "Well, this is going

to be an exception," she said tersely. "Because there's no way my parents would let me keep seeing Manuel if they found out. And, Jeanie, I can't give him up!"

Jeanie was silent. "Well, you'd better find Liz then," she suggested. "And you'd better do it in the morning."

Sandra frowned. Jeanie was right. She was going to have to find Elizabeth before first period and make sure there was absolutely no mention of her and Manuel. Not that week, and not ever.

Four

"Liz," Sandra exclaimed, hurrying up to Elizabeth the following morning before class. Elizabeth looked up with a smile. She had just been thinking about Sandra, having just proofread her column for the week, in which she had mentioned Manuel and Sandra.

"Hi, Sandy," she said. She looked at the girl with admiration, thinking how much prettier and more animated Sandra seemed since she and Manuel had gotten together. "How are you? I haven't seen you in ages."

"Liz," Sandra said again, looking distraught, "we have to talk. Is there any chance I can drag you off somewhere alone for a minute or two before school starts?"

Elizabeth looked down at the large envelope she was holding. "Actually, I was hoping to get these proofs to Mr. Collins before class. The 'Eyes and Ears' column needs to be dummied up this morning."

Sandra looked at the envelope with alarm. "That's exactly what I wanted to talk to you about. Please, Liz," she added, upset. "This is serious."

Elizabeth noticed how flushed Sandra's cheeks were and how agitated she seemed. "Let's go into the lounge where we can be alone," she suggested. She would have to explain to Mr. Collins why the page proofs were late, as it was obvious that Sandra really needed to talk. Elizabeth was more than a little puzzled. What could Sandra have to talk about to her? It wasn't as if they knew each other all that well.

"I bumped into Manuel outside school this morning. He looks so happy," Elizabeth said, trying to make conversation as they headed together into the student lounge.

Sandra nodded, distracted. "Yes, we both are," she said. "As a matter of fact, Liz, that's partly what I wanted to talk to you about. Manuel and I both feel kind of shy about things. And we'd prefer it if you wouldn't mention anything about us in your column."

Elizabeth laughed. "Oh, is that what's bothering you? Sandy, you know the column isn't serious. It's all meant to be taken in good spirits. And besides, the comment about you and Manuel is incredibly innocent. Here, I can read it to you." She took the page proofs out of the manila envelope and scanned until she found the excerpt in question. She read it out loud. "That's it," she said when she finished. "Not exactly incriminating." She put the proofs away again.

Sandra looked pale. "Liz, I really can't let you print that," she said nervously. "Would it be a big deal to take it out and write about someone else instead?"

Elizabeth looked at her thoughtfully. "Well, it's already in page proofs. I don't like to make major changes at this point. Is it really that important that it come out?"

"Yes," Sandra said. "To me, it *is* that important."

Elizabeth couldn't understand why Sandra was objecting to having her name linked with Manuel's. Just about everyone in school knew about them already. "If you really feel strongly about it, I can take it out," she said at last. "But to tell you the truth, Sandy, I don't see why it bothers you. I haven't said anything that's really embarrassing or untrue, have I?"

"No," Sandra said quietly. "I guess not." She was silent for a minute, deep in thought. "It's just that I really don't want a lot of people finding out about Manuel and me, that's all!" she blurted out almost hysterically.

Elizabeth stared at her. "Why not?" "I remember when Jeffrey and I started going out, I used to get a little embarrassed sometimes when people teased us. But I liked it, too." She smiled, thinking back. "I guess it made me feel kind of proud, knowing people were thinking of us as a couple."

Sandra's eyes filled with tears, and she looked away. "Yeah. I can see how you'd feel that way," she murmured. "I wish. . . ." Her voice trailed off uncertainly.

"You wish what?" Elizabeth prompted quietly. Something told her to go gently, that this was a very delicate subject for Sandra.

"I wish I could brag to everyone about Manuel," Sandra said. "But, Liz, I can't. The truth is that there's a very good reason why I prefer to keep our relationship quiet for a while. Do me a favor. Help me out and cut that passage from the column."

"OK," Elizabeth said. She drew a line through the offending sentences, determined not to press Sandra to explain herself. It was obvious from the girl's expression that this was a painful subject for her, and Elizabeth didn't want to interfere. But Sandra didn't change the subject or make an excuse to leave the lounge, as Elizabeth had expected. Instead she looked helplessly at Elizabeth, her eyes shining with unshed tears.

"I know you must think I'm a complete jerk," she said defensively. "I know how bad it looks, like I'm ashamed of Manuel or something. But that isn't how it is at all.

"It's just that my parents . . ." Sandra drooped visibly. "Oh, Liz, what would you do if your parents objected to Jeffrey for some reason? If they made it clear to you that he was from the wrong sort of family or that they had some reason for thinking he wasn't suitable for you to go out with?"

"I can't imagine my parents objecting," Elizabeth said. "You mean about something like his religion or family background, right?"

Sandra nodded, and a single tear spilled down her cheek.

"'Are you saying that your parents—" Elizabeth stared at Sandra. "Sandy, do you mean that you want to keep your relationship with Manuel a secret because your parents would object to the fact that he's Mexican?"

Sandra nodded. "I'm so ashamed of them," she whispered. "But, Liz, I love them. They're my parents. They've always been a little over-protective of me because I'm their only daughter and their youngest child. But they've always trusted me. I've never given them any reason not to."

"So they don't know about Manuel?"

Sandra shook her head. "They've made it

43

clear how they'd react if they *did* know, though. I've tested them a few times. I've broached the subject of Mexican-Americans and I've even asked my mom outright what she'd do if I fell in love with a Mexican." She winced. "You should've seen the look on her face. It was as if I'd asked her about someone who had the plague."

Elizabeth was quiet as she thought this over. She sympathized with Sandra's problem. She couldn't imagine her own parents ever being prejudiced in this way, but suppose they were, and suppose she had fallen in love with someone they disapproved of? What on earth would she have done? Sneaking around behind her parents' backs was clearly causing Sandra's real torment.

"Maybe some of their objections would disappear if they got the chance to meet Manuel," Elizabeth said thoughtfully. "It seems to me that most people's prejudices grow out of ignorance. I'm sure once they met him—"

"But you see, they've already convinced themselves that Mexicans are different, undesirable. I know if they met Manuel, they'd be studying him, trying to prove they were right. It would be awful." Sandra seemed so upset at the thought that Elizabeth's heart went out to her.

But she still felt there was only one possible solution to the problem. "Look," Elizabeth said.

44

"Your parents are wrong, but the truth is, I don't think what you're doing is right, either. Sneaking around and refusing to help them to get to know Manuel is really feeding into their prejudice. You need to face up to them, Sandy. Tell them you have a friend you want them to meet and just invite Manuel over. Give them a chance. Who knows, maybe they'll really surprise you."

Sandra winced. "I've never done anything to disappoint them before," she whispered. "I can't imagine having the guts to stand up to them on something this big."

"Well," Elizabeth said with a sigh, "I don't think you've got much choice, Sandy. If you're asking for advice, I think you've got to tell them. You're only going to hurt Manuel and yourself by carrying on this way."

"I suppose so," Sandra said weakly.

"Besides," Elizabeth added, "you have to remember that your parents grew up in a different era. They may have ideas that are wrong, but you can help them, Sandy. If you don't, who will?"

Sandra sighed unhappily. "I guess you're right," she murmured. "Anyway, Manuel is really upset about all this. He wants me to invite him over so they can meet him. He's incredibly proper about certain things, and he feels that it's wrong for us to go out when he hasn't met my family."

"He's right," Elizabeth said firmly. "Sandy, the more I hear about Manuel, the more I like him!"

"That's how I feel, too," Sandra said sadly. "And that's exactly why I'm afraid to introduce him to my parents, Liz. I'm afraid they'll force me to give him up."

"I didn't think about that side of it," Elizabeth said honestly. She could see why Sandra was worried. Elizabeth knew that prejudices were very hard to shake. And who knew what reaction the Bacons might have when they discovered that their only daughter had fallen in love with someone they considered wrong for her?

"This lunch," Amy Sutton said, pushing her tray away in disgust, "is enough to make dieting seem fun. Can't they do anything about the food around here?"

"Daddy sent me a postcard saying the food in Rome is divine," Lila remarked, busily finishing the last bites of a gourmet chocolate ice-cream bar. "And speaking of Daddy, he says he's gotten me the best birthday presents ever. He called the other night to ask what colors I like best."

Amy rolled her eyes at Jessica. The group

assembled around the lunch table—Amy Sutton, Cara Walker, Jeanie West, Sandy Bacon, and Jessica—was used to hearing Lila brag about her father's extravagance.

"Speaking of birthdays," Lila added, setting her elbows casually on the table and looking around at the others, "I know you guys have probably all been wondering what I'd like, you know, in the way of a party. I mean, I know you've probably all been talking about it a lot and everything."

"Cara, did you find out anything more about that British rock group you said was coming to the Westwood Stadium a week from Saturday?" Jessica asked casually. "I know you thought you could get tickets, and Steven mentioned you might want to get a little group together."

Cara glanced at Lila, who looked very upset, then back at Jessica. Clearly Jessica's plan to make it seem that no one cared about Lila's birthday was working.

"Well, there *may* be tickets," she said vaguely.

Lila drew in a long, quivery breath. "I guess a rock concert might be fun, *before* a big party," she said.

"And then, didn't you mention going on and doing something afterward?" Amy pressed Cara, taking her cue from Jessica. "Only you don't have very many tickets, do you? Just enough for a few of us, right?"

47

"Well," Cara said faintly, wetting her lips and watching nervously for Lila's reaction, "we're—uh, we're not sure."

"You guys, cut it out," Lila moaned, unable to stand it anymore. "I know you're just doing this to torture me!"

"Doing what?" Amy demanded with mock innocence. "Lila, what are you talking about?"

"You know," Lila faltered. "Acting like you don't even care that it's my birthday!"

"Lila," Jessica said with exaggerated patience, "nobody even *thinks* about birthdays any more. That's so *babyish*."

Lila turned the stick from her ice-cream bar over and over again. "Well, my birthday *is* important," she said at last.

"Are you kidding?" Amy burst out. "Jess is right, Lila. Birthdays are incredibly boring. The only thing to do is forget you're even having one. Anything else is just totally uncool."

Lila looked positively miserable, and Jessica felt a tiny twinge of guilt. But it would be worth it, she reminded herself. Lila would be honestly surprised by the party they threw for her the day after her birthday. And in the meantime maybe she'd tone down her bragging about all the wonderful presents her father was buying her!

"Hey," Amy said suddenly, "I almost forgot

48

to ask you all about this, but I heard there's a big dance coming up at the country club. Are you all going to go?"

"It's not for a couple of weeks," Jessica said, looking bored. "I have to wait and see if there's anyone I feel like going with."

"What about you, Sandy?" Amy demanded. "It should be fun. You can go with Manuel."

Sandra reddened. "Oh, I don't know," she said. "I'm not sure I really want to go that much. The country club is so—you know, sort of *stuffy*."

"Well, you can't expect too much," Lila said, trying to keep her spirits up. "After all, this is Sweet Valley, not Rome. But I think it's actually a fairly nice place for a dance."

"Well," Sandra said, getting to her feet and balling up her lunch bag, "I guess so. But I'm not planning on going anyway." She waved at Manuel, who had just entered the lunchroom over by the patio doors. "I've got to run. I'll see you guys later."

"Hmm," Amy said, watching her go. "I wonder if Sandy thinks the country club is too stuffy for *her*—or too stuffy for Manuel Lopez."

"That's not a nice thing to say, Amy," Jeanie said in a frosty voice, picking up her tray and getting up from the table.

"What did I say?" Amy demanded as Jeanie walked off.

Jessica shrugged. She wasn't sure why Jeanie had been so touchy. But it seemed to her that tempers had been more than a little strained since Sandra and Manuel had started going out.

Sandra glanced impatiently at her watch. It was twenty minutes to eight on Friday evening, and she was waiting on the street corner for Manuel to pick her up. They were going over to his cousin's house for the long-awaited party where she would get to meet all his relatives—that is, his cousins and grandparents and uncles and aunts. It was drizzling a little, and Sandra knew her hair was going to frizz. If only Manuel could just pick her up at her house! She hated sneaking around like this. And it had been harder than ever to get away that evening. Her mother seemed suspicious when she said she was meeting a bunch of friends at Casey's Place, an ice-cream parlor in the mall. She kept asking who was driving and why she had to walk over to Enid's house to get picked up.

Of course her mother was right to suspect her, Sandra thought. She wasn't used to lying—she probably hadn't sounded convincing. *Nothing like a guilty conscience*, she thought ruefully. Her face brightened when she saw Manuel's car approaching.

"Look at you!" he cried as she got in the car. "Sandy, you're all wet! Why didn't you—" His voice broke off, and he looked away. "Sorry," he said bitterly. "I forgot. No Mexicans welcome at the Bacon household, right?"

"Please," Sandra said, taking a comb from her purse and trying to straighten her damp hair. "Look, Manuel, I feel as rotten as you do, having to sneak around like this." She bit her lip. "In fact I feel a lot worse." She seemed so miserable that Manuel relented a little.

"I just hate to see you standing out here on the street," he said unhappily. "I've been raised to be a gentleman. And a gentleman picks a lady up at her house and doesn't let her stand out in the rain!"

Sandra tried to make a joke out of the situation, but it was clear Manuel didn't find it amusing. She didn't really blame him, either. Even worse, lying to her parents made her feel very guilty. She could barely look forward to the evening when it had begun so badly.

Clearly something was going to have to change. The question was, what?

Five

It was a perfect day for a picnic, a warm and sunny Saturday afternoon, but so far the Bacons' barbecue with the Wests was not going very well.

Sandra was a nervous wreck. Every time her mother and Mrs. West started to talk, she was convinced something incriminating would be revealed. "It's so nice that Jeanie and Sandy have been able to spend so much time together lately," Mrs. Bacon said at one point.

Jeanie coughed. "By the way," she interrupted, clearly trying to change the subject, "did I tell you that Sandy and I have been trying to brainstorm for new ideas to raise money for the Regina Morrow Scholarship Fund?"

Sandra pretended to be very busy grilling hot dogs. "Yeah," she confirmed. "The cheerleaders are getting really involved. We have to practice almost twice as much as we used to. Don't we, Jeanie?''

"Uh—yes," Jeanie said awkwardly. She gave Sandra a pleading look. Helping her friend cover up her romance was proving to be a much more treacherous business than she had imagined. "Sandy," she said, watching her friend turn the hot dogs, "want to take a quick walk?"

"Don't be long, you two," Mr. West admonished. "We're almost ready to eat."

"That's right," Mrs. Bacon seconded, taking Sandra's place at the grill. "You two have spent enough time together over the past few weeks as it is. We'd like to share a little of your company this afternoon, if you don't mind!"

"Phew." Sandra breathed a sigh of relief as the two girls retreated from the small picnic table area to stroll down to the edge of Secca Lake, the spot they had chosen for their outing. "I'm sorry about that," she said. "I hate putting you in the position of having to cover for me."

Jeanie frowned. "To be honest, San, I don't like it either. I think you should tell your parents the truth."

Sandra didn't say anything at first. Then she nodded. "I know I should, Jeanie. I feel awful about what I've been doing. And last night I met all of Manuel's relatives. They were so nice to me, too. I really do want him to be able to meet my family. As a matter of fact," she said resolutely, "the first chance I get, I'm going to talk to my mom."

Sandra took a deep breath. They had just gotten home from the picnic, and she had decided that now would be the best time for a long talk with her mother. Mrs. Bacon was busy in the garden, pruning the beautiful azalea bushes that were her pride and joy. *She should be in a good mood now*, Sandra thought. This was the perfect moment to tell her the truth about Manuel.

"Hi, honey!" Mrs. Bacon said, sitting back and smiling at her daughter as Sandra came outside and plopped down beside her on the grass. Mrs. Bacon squinted up at the sky. "Isn't it a gorgeous afternoon? Today was a perfect day for the picnic."

"Mmm," Sandra agreed, watching with admiration as her mother deftly pruned back the brightly flowering bushes. Her mother was so good at everything! It was one of the reasons that Sandra was slightly in awe of her, and more than a little afraid to tell her what was on her mind.

"What are you doing tonight? Are you going

out?" her mother asked curiously. Mrs. Bacon had always been interested in Sandra's plans and loved to hear about her activities with her friends. Sandra never really noticed until recently how involved her mother was in her life. Now that she had something to hide, it was painfully obvious.

"Oh, I guess so," she said vaguely. "A bunch of us were talking about meeting at the Dairi Burger or something. Maybe seeing a movie afterward or going back to someone's house to watch a movie on tape." She shrugged, trying hard to seem nonchalant. Actually she *was* going to the popular hamburger hangout, but the only person she planned to meet there was Manuel.

"You know, you're welcome to bring your friends back here," Mrs. Bacon said, snipping off a stray twig from one of the bushes. "You know how much your father and I enjoy getting to know your friends."

Yeah, Sandra thought. If her mother only knew! Surely Manuel would be the one friend they wouldn't welcome with open arms. She took a deep breath. She had promised herself that she was going to talk to her mother, and it wasn't going to do any good to stall. "Mom," she said slowly, "did you ever think about what would happen if—well, suppose I were to meet somebody and fall in love. Only he wasn't exactly the sort of guy you and Daddy had in mind for me, say, maybe he was from a very different background. Would you mind?"

"Honey, I only want you to be happy," Mrs. Bacon said seriously. "You know how much your father and I want you to have friends you care about. But we also hope that they'll be the right sort of friends, people who have the kind of upbringing you've had. Doesn't that make sense to you? We just don't want to see you make things hard for yourself."

Sandra bit her lip. This was even harder than she had expected. "But suppose I did," she pressed. "And suppose the guy was—well, you know—different."

"Sandy, this all sounds like an awful lot of supposing to me," Mrs. Bacon said in the no-nonsense tone that Sandra knew and dreaded. "But I'll tell you this. I've seen a lot of relationships start up and falter in my day, and there's a lot of truth to what *my* mother used to tell me. Two people who fall in love have enough problems ahead of them without compounding the issue. You can count on the fact that two people from different backgrounds are going to have ten strikes against them from the start. Why make it harder for yourself?"

Sandra stared at her. "But suppose," she said faintly, "that I really fell in love—I mean *really*—

56

and thought it was worth working harder to make up for those differences?"

Mrs. Bacon frowned. "If that ever happened, I think I would have to tell you the truth. Sandy, my feeling is just like Grandma's. You know the old proverb about birds of a feather flocking together. I just don't see the point in making your life harder than it has to be."

Sandra blinked back tears. "I think you're wrong," she said suddenly, startled by the vehemence in her voice. "I think when two people fall in love, it happens for a whole bunch of different reasons. I don't think it's something that you can plan, like choosing a college, or a job, or something. It's like"—she faltered briefly— "like magic," she finished helplessly. "And if the two people happen to be from different backgrounds, then that's all there is to it."

Mrs. Bacon looked closely at Sandra. "Honey, who's been telling you these things? Have you been watching too many romantic movies? I can't remember you ever talking like this before."

Sandra felt exasperated. Why was it so hard to talk to her mother? All these years she'd thought they had such a great relationship. Now, when she really needed to unburden herself, she found it was impossible to say what she really meant.

"Maybe I'm changing," she said helplessly.

She didn't sound very convincing, even to herself.

"Well, it's fine to think hard about these things. Just remember, it's one thing to hypothesize, and it's quite another to actually get involved with someone from a different background," Mrs. Bacon said firmly, picking up her gardening shears. She was still frowning. "Honey, I don't know where you're getting all these ideas about falling in love and meeting someone from a different background. But I have to tell you that I don't like the sound of it." She shook her head. "Your father and I want you to meet nice people, Sandy, like that boy, Carl Pierce, at the club. Like Jeanie and your other friends. And why should we worry about some kind of hypothetical problem?" She went back to snipping the azaleas. "In fact, I have to say that I was thinking last night about what you asked me the other day, when you were talking about what would happen if you fell in love with a Mexican boy. I got so upset I couldn't sleep. Sandy, if that really happened, I don't know what I'd do."

Sandra felt all her courage ebb. *I'm a coward*, she thought with disgust. *I just can't stand up to my mother*.

She knew she was letting Manuel down, but she couldn't tell her mother the truth. Not yet.

58

She'd just have to do her best to explain to Manuel that she needed a little more time.

"Hey," Manuel said, leaning across the table and covering Sandy's hand with his. It was later that evening, and they were sitting in the back of the Dairi Burger at what they now considered to be "their" booth. "What's up? You haven't even touched your hamburger. And I happen to know it's the specialty of the house."

Sandra smiled. One of the things she liked so much about Manuel was that he was almost always in a good mood. And he always noticed her mood, too. If she was the slightest bit down or depressed, he picked up on it right away and tried to cheer her. "We had a picnic this afternoon," she told him. "I'm not really that hungry."

Manuel was quiet for a minute, as if trying to decide whether or not to broach the subject they had tacitly dropped since the previous evening. "Anything to do with your parents?" he asked with feigned nonchalance. "Did they give you a hard time when you told them about us?"

Sandra reddened slightly. "No," she murmured.

"Hey, that's great!" Manuel said, clasping her hands tightly. "That calls for a celebration!"

"Manuel," Sandra said painfully, "they didn't give me a hard time because I didn't tell them— yet," she added quickly, seeing his face fall.

"Sandy, you promised." Manuel pushed his plate away with an angry gesture that made her stomach feel hollow.

Sandy had never seen him angry before, and she had a sudden terrible fear that he might storm off and never come back. "I'm sorry!" she cried. "Manuel, I really meant to talk to my mother this afternoon. I honestly did. I tried, too, but it was just impossible. It was like coming up against a brick wall."

"Sandy, we can't go on like this," Manuel said, his expression tortured. "Do you have any idea how rotten it makes me feel, having to sneak around all the time, meeting you places instead of being able to come pick you up? It makes me feel really low—like some kind of second-class citizen." He stared at her, hurt. "It makes me feel you're ashamed of me."

"Manuel, that isn't true!" Sandra said helplessly. "I'm crazy about you. The truth is, I found out something terrible this afternoon. I guess I've lived my whole life exactly the way my parents had mapped it out for me. It never occurred to me to question any of their values. Now, for the first time, I have to face the fact that they're wrong. Really wrong. I know in my heart that what you and I feel for each other is wonderful. And there's no way I'm going to give it up."

"You keep saying that," Manuel objected, "but when it comes right down to it, you aren't willing to talk to them. How can you possibly expect them to change unless you help them?"

"You sound like Liz." Sandra sighed. "Manuel, it isn't that easy. You don't know what it's like being the only child left at home. My parents are just amazingly protective of me. They act like it's a big deal if I want to see a movie that they don't want me to see. Can you imagine how they're going to handle a major disagreement like this?"

Manuel looked searchingly at her. "No," he said at last. "I guess I can't. But I know one thing. You and I can't last this way. And if you're serious about not giving up what we've got, you're going to have to stand up to them. I'm willing to wait, but not forever."

"Just wait for a little while longer," Sandra pleaded. "Please, Manuel."

Manuel stared down at their hands, which were still clasped. "Well," he said, relenting a little, "I guess I can see how it might be hard for you." He shrugged. "My mom always says that it takes a lot of inches to make up a mile.

Be patient, she tells me. Just take the inches, and the mile will come in time."

Sandra squeezed his hand tightly. "I promise to talk to them as soon as I can," she whispered. She stared down at their intertwined fingers. wishing she could think of some way to make it up to Manuel. Suddenly she remembered his asking about her motorboat the previous week. "I don't suppose you're still interested in going boating sometime?" she asked in a teasing voice. "Or were you just pretending to be interested back when we hardly knew each other?"

Manuel laughed. "You've got a lot of nerve. You know how much I want to take you out in your boat," he declared. Manuel had a lot of experience with boats the summer before, when he had had a job at the Secca Lake boathouse, where the Bacons kept the little speedboat that Sandra had gotten for her last birthday.

"Well? What about next week?" she asked, cupping his hand in hers.

Manuel's face lit up for a moment. "But you'd have to tell your parents," he said, frowning again. "And I don't want to put any more pressure on you than I have already."

Sandra thought fast. It was true that her parents wouldn't let her go out in the boat by herself. She'd have to tell them she was going with a friend. She could always say she was going with Jeanie, though.

"I don't mind," she said rapidly. From the grateful smile on Manuel's face, she knew he had misunderstood, and she deliberately let him. Why break his heart by telling him she intended, once again, to lie and say she was taking Jeanie?

"Sandy, I love you," Manuel said earnestly.

Her heartbeat quickened. "I love you, too," she whispered.

The magic of that moment made it all worthwhile. For the first time, Sandra was convinced everything was really going to work out just the way she hoped. Her parents would understand. They just had to!

Six

"Now, remember," Jessica advised in a low voice on Tuesday morning as she spotted Lila sauntering toward the small group assembled on the lawn, "we've all got plans for next Saturday night. And we all think Lila is being a baby, making such a big deal out of a birthday. OK?"

Amy nodded vehemently. "She's going to have a fit!" she predicted gleefully.

Cara and Jeanie exchanged glances. "If I know Lila," Cara said, "a *fit* is an understatement for what she's going to have. She's been on the rampage for days about the fact that we're not taking her birthday seriously enough. Something tells me she's about to give us all a piece of her mind."

"Big deal," Amy said, shrugging. "Lila's got to lighten up. She has to learn to take a joke."

Jessica grinned. Listening to Amy Sutton now, it was hard to believe the blonde had ever been her twin sister's best friend. In sixth grade, Amy had been much more like Elizabeth than like Jessica. When the Suttons moved to Connecticut, Elizabeth had been heartbroken. The ironic thing was that when they moved back, just a few months ago, Amy was a totally different person. Even Jessica had to admit that Amy tended to be on the vain side now. And boy crazy! There wasn't a single guy at school she hadn't examined from every angle, though her new theory was that they were all hopelessly immature. Her latest involvement—with Bruce Patman, a good-looking, dark-haired senior who was known to be the richest boy at school—had caused a real scandal. Bruce had been Regina Morrow's boyfriend before Amy, and though, strictly speaking, it wasn't Amy's fault that Bruce left Regina, she had certainly been partially responsible. And it was soon after the break-up that Regina had turned to the crowd who had introduced her to the drugs that proved, tragically, to be fatal for her. Elizabeth and Amy were barely polite to each other now, and Jessica, who hadn't been all that thrilled to hear she was moving back, was one of her chief supporters. She especially liked the fact that Amy wasn't going to put up with any of Lila's nonsense.

But actually Lila seemed quiet and subdued when she joined the group under the shade trees.

"Hey, Lila," Amy said, nudging Jessica in the ribs. "That looks like a new sweater. Is it?"

"Yeah," Lila said listlessly. "Daddy came back from Rome last night, and he gave me a few presents. You know, sort of homecoming presents. He's saving most of them for my birthday, though, remember, a week from Saturday?"

"Oh, yeah," Amy said, studying the sweater with interest. "Well, it's really pretty, Lila."

"Which reminds me," Lila said, looking around at her friends with obvious anxiety. "I know this probably sounds really stupid, because I know you guys are planning some kind of surprise party for that night, but I just thought I'd mention it. Daddy wants to take me out to Jacques', a new French bistro in San Mirabel, but I told him that I was practically positive you guys were planning something. In secret," she concluded.

"Planning something?" Jessica echoed, her expression blank. "What do you mean?"

"I'm only bringing it up so we don't make a real mess of everything," Lila pointed out patiently. "I mean, what if Daddy makes the reservations and then we have to cancel? Unless," she said suddenly, her eyes brightening, "you guys have got my dad in on the whole thing. Is that it? So going to Jacques' is really just a ploy?"

"Amy," Jessica said with mock confusion, "do *you* know what she's talking about? I feel like I'm missing something here."

"No idea," Amy said, enjoying herself. "Lila, do us a favor and just talk in plain English. What on earth are you trying to say?"

"Do you mean to tell me," Lila asked between clenched teeth, "that you *aren't* planning anything for that night? After all the times I've given parties for you?"

"Well, we hadn't *planned* anything," Jessica said thoughtfully. "But that's because we all think birthdays are kind of silly, Li. Think about it. By the time you reach a certain age, there just doesn't seem to be much point in making a big fuss."

"I am not *old*," Lila said coldly.

"I guess we could do *something*," Jessica said doubtfully.

"Except we all kind of forgot about it, to tell you the truth, and now we've all got plans. Remember, Cara got us tickets to go see the Boys at Westwood."

Lila's eyes flashed. "You're not really serious about that, are you? You mean you're really all going to get together and go out—on my birthday—and not even invite me?"

"You said you hated rock concerts," Amy said mildly.

"And Cara could only get four tickets," Jessica added. "But we'll make it up to you, Li. We'll take you out for ice cream, or something, the next day."

Lila got to her feet, her face red. "Ice cream!" she snapped. "That's great. That's really great. After all the times I've knocked myself out throwing parties. I guess when it comes to something like this, you really find out who your friends are."

"Lila, don't make a scene," Jessica admonished. "People are *staring*!"

"I couldn't care less," Lila said bitterly, spinning on her heel and stomping off. "I never want to speak to any of you again as long as I live!" she called over her shoulder.

"Wow," Amy said appreciatively. "Real fireworks!"

"Jessica, do you think she'll ever forgive us?" Cara asked anxiously. "She does have a point. I mean, she's always giving parties at her place. And it *is* her birthday."

"Oh, she'll get over it. She'll forgive us the minute she sees the fantastic party we've put together for Sunday night," Jessica assured her.

"I don't know," Jeanie said doubtfully. "She really looked mad, Jess."

Jessica didn't answer. It was true. Lila *had* reacted more strongly than she had expected.

But that was the thing about Lila Fowler. They could count on the fact that she wouldn't stay mad forever. They were all just going to have to try harder to ensure that her surprise party was the best birthday celebration in Sweet Valley history!

Jessica and Cara Walker were hard at work on Lila's birthday banner in the student lounge when Elizabeth and Enid came in. "What's that?" Elizabeth asked her twin, coming over to inspect their handiwork.

"It's supposed to be like a trade union banner. Each panel is going to represent a different aspect of Lila's life," Jessica said proudly. "See, this panel is 'Lila Shopping.' See all the different outfits we've got painted already? The next is 'Lila Giving Parties.' This is supposed to be Fowler Crest."

Elizabeth giggled as she stepped back to survey the enormous banner. "What if she finds it? Where are you guys hiding something that big?"

"We're keeping it in the art room. Don't worry, we've got Lila under control," Jessica said serenely.

Enid sat down on a couch, her expression thoughtful as she took an envelope out of her notebook. "My grandmother's latest letter," she murmured to Elizabeth. "Believe it or not, I haven't had time to read it yet. And I got it yesterday!"

"How is your grandmother?" Elizabeth asked with concern. She knew that, since her grandfather had died, Enid had been particularly worried about her grandmother, who lived alone in Chicago. It had only been a few months since his death, and Enid and her mother were concerned about what would be the most sensible step to take next.

Enid opened the letter and scanned the first few lines. "She sounds so lonesome," she said sadly. "I think I'm going to suggest to my mother that we ask her to move in with us."

"Where would you put her?" Jessica cut in, oblivious to the fact that Enid was talking only to Elizabeth.

Enid shrugged. "I know our house isn't big, but Nana is so wonderful. It would be worth crowding a little. Besides, I hate to think of her in Chicago all by herself. She must be very lonely."

Jessica rolled her eyes. "Much as I love my grandparents, I sure wouldn't be thrilled if they moved in. Our house is too crowded as it is.

Luckily I can keep some of my clothes in Steven's closet."

Elizabeth groaned. "Our hearts are bleeding for you, Jess," she said dryly. She turned back to her friend. "I think your idea is wonderful, Enid. And I bet your mother would be completely behind it if you wrote to your grandmother and asked her to think about moving out here."

Enid jumped up, her eyes sparkling. "I'm going to bring it up first thing when I get home!" she declared. "I bet you're right, Elizabeth. I bet my mom will be absolutely thrilled, if she hasn't already thought of the same thing herself."

"Jeanie," Sandra called, hurrying up to her friend outside the gym. Sandra had been trying to find Jeanie all day. She wanted to ask her if she could tell her mother that she was taking her out in her boat that afternoon. She had already promised Manuel that they could go that day after school, and he'd arranged to get off work. Now she just needed to supply her mother with a name, and Jeanie's was the most logical.

"Hi, Sandy," Jeanie said nonchalantly, leaning over to straighten her sock. "How are you? I've barely seen you the last two days. In fact, I don't think I've talked to you since the picnic on Saturday."

Sandra winced. "Yeah, thanks again for covering for me," she said. "I didn't expect my mother to grill you like that. Honestly, Jeanie, I think she's starting to suspect that I haven't been telling her the whole truth."

"In fact, you haven't been telling her the truth at all," Jeanie corrected her.

Sandra bit her lip. It wasn't like Jeanie to sound so critical. "You're not mad at me, are you?" she asked anxiously. "I guess I put you in kind of a difficult position, having to lie for me." In fact, the barbecue had been a strain for both girls, as Mrs. Bacon had referred repeatedly to events the two had supposedly been to together.

"Look, what you do with Manuel is your business. Frankly, I think you're wrong not to tell your parents the truth. It's only going to backfire in the long run. And it's got to be hurtful to Manuel in the meantime."

"I keep trying to talk to them, Jeanie," Sandra said, upset. "But you know how conservative they are! They're going to have a fit when they find out."

Jean shrugged. "Well, it's up to you. But I want to ask you a favor, Sandy. Leave me out from now on. I feel uncomfortable having to cover for you. It's too hard with our mothers always talking to each other."

Sandra stared at her. This wasn't what she had expected at all. Now what was she supposed to do? She could hardly tell her mother she was going out on the boat with a boy she had never introduced to them. And she couldn't say she was going alone. The rule was she had to have someone with her whenever she went out in the boat.

"I won't ask you to lie for me anymore," Sandra said carefully, stalling for time. Suddenly an idea struck her. Why not invite Jeanie along with them? That way she wouldn't be lying when she told her mother that she had gone out with Jeanie. "What are you doing after school?" she asked. "Have you got plans? I was going to take Manuel out in the boat, and I was thinking you might want to come with us."

"Sorry," Jeanie said, "but Tom and I are meeting his brother at the beach." She regarded her friend. "Anyway, you don't really want me along. You just want me to cover for you so that you can tell your mom you were with me again."

"That isn't fair," Sandra said weakly. But she knew Jeanie was right. She wasn't used to lying, and she felt terrible as she watched her friend walk away. Jeanie had seen right through her.

Now what was she supposed to do?

"Hi, Sandy," Elizabeth said cheerfully, coming out of the *Oracle* office with her arms full of paste-up boards. She had been finishing up a project for Mr. Collins and was eager to get outside for some fresh air now that the school day was over. "How are things? Did you notice I cut that thing about you and Manuel from the 'Eyes and Ears' column?"

Sandra nodded. "Thanks, Liz." She looked thoughtfully down at the boards. "You working this afternoon?" she asked somewhat wistfully.

"Nope. I'm all through," Elizabeth said with a smile. "Actually, I can't wait to get outside. It's so gorgeous today, and I feel like I've been cooped up inside for days." She fell in step beside Sandra. "What are you up to this afternoon? Don't you have cheerleading practice?"

"No," Sandra said. "Not today. Ricky called a rest day. He thinks we're all looking a little low-energy."

As a matter of fact, Elizabeth thought, Sandra didn't look all that great. There were faint shadows under her eyes, and she looked tired.

"Hey," Sandra said suddenly, "why don't

you come out to Secca Lake with Manuel and me? We're planning on taking my little speedboat out."

"That sounds fun," Elizabeth said. "But wouldn't you two rather be by yourselves?"

"No," Sandra said quickly. "I mean, yes, but not all the time. Not this afternoon."

Elizabeth laughed. "Why? I always thought going out on a boat on a beautiful afternoon was supposed to feature *two* people, not three."

Sandra was warming to the idea. "Please come," she begged. "I really want you to get a chance to know Manuel better. Come on, Liz. Manuel really wants you to come, too." This last comment couldn't have been farther from the truth, but Sandra figured she would have plenty of time to convince Manuel that Elizabeth would make the outing even more fun.

"Well," Elizabeth said uncertainly. It really was a beautiful afternoon, and she hadn't been out to Secca Lake in a while. And she loved motorboats. "OK," she said with a smile. "As long as you're sure Manuel won't think I'm cramping your style." She looked ruefully down at her denim skirt. "But we'll have to stop by my house so I can change into my swimsuit, OK?"

"Sure!" Sandra said happily. "Let me go find Manuel, and we'll meet you in front of the school. I've got my mom's Toyota today."

75

Elizabeth smiled to herself as she watched Sandra hurry away. Nothing like love to make someone seem a little loopy, she told herself. And Sandra Bacon really hadn't seemed quite herself since she had fallen in love with Manuel.

"I thought the whole point was for us to have a chance to do something special, just the two of us," Manuel said.

"I couldn't help it, Manuel. It was stupid of me to have mentioned it in the first place, but it just kind of slipped out. And it was obvious she wanted to come. I *had* to ask her!"

Manuel frowned. "I don't suppose this has anything to do with the fact that now you can tell your mother you went boating with Liz, does it?"

Sandra felt her stomach turn over. She felt a rush of conflicting emotions: sorrow at hurting Manuel; an urge to protect him; an urge to defend herself; guilt that she was lying, again. "Please," she said softly, putting her hand on his arm, "let's not fight again. I hate it so much when you get mad at me, Manuel. It just cuts me to pieces inside."

"How do you think it makes me feel?"

"Let's just go have a good time," she said warmly. "Liz won't stop us from having fun and enjoying each other's company, will she?"

"I guess not," Manuel mumbled.

Sandra looked at him anxiously. He really wasn't his usual good-natured self lately. In fact he seemed tense and withdrawn. She stroked his arm uncertainly, wishing there was something she could say or do to make everything all right. She knew, though, that what Manuel wanted from her was just impossible at this point. She couldn't bear to face her parents.

"I promise," she said in a low voice, "that we'll really have a good time this afternoon. I know I've been hard to deal with lately. I've been worrying about a lot of stuff, and it's making me a little crazy."

Manuel squeezed her arm, flashing her one of his wonderful, sympathetic smiles. "Just hang in there," he said softly. "And don't worry about me, Sandy. I'm incredibly patient when it comes to something important. Something like *us.*"

She smiled, tears glistening in her eyes. "You're an amazing guy," she said softly, leaning over to trace his lips with her finger. "I don't think I could stand it if anything were to come between us."

Manuel was quiet, and Sandra slipped her arms around his neck and kissed him gently. For some reason she felt uneasy, as if something were still unsettled. But she pushed the thought away. Trying to appear lighthearted, she led Manuel off to the parking lot to look for Elizabeth.

Mrs. Wakefield had taken the day off from her interior design business, and she was in the kitchen when Elizabeth, Sandra, and Manuel came trooping in fifteen minutes later. "Hi, Mom!" Elizabeth said, giving her an affectionate kiss on the cheek. "Mom, this is Sandy Bacon and Manuel Lopez. We're all going boating together at Secca Lake. I'm just going to run up and get my suit."

Mrs. Wakefield smiled. "Fine. That'll give me a chance to get to know your friends," she said. "Would either of you like some iced tea?" she asked Sandra and Manuel.

"Yes, please," they said at the same time, smiling self-consciously at each other.

"Now, Sandy Bacon is a familiar name to me from the cheerleading squad. But Manuel Lopez . . . I don't think I know that name." Mrs. Wakefield continued to smile. "Are you a junior, too?"

Manuel nodded. "But not a cheerleader," he joked. "I keep my efforts confined to the track field."

Mrs. Wakefield laughed. "And where do you live, Manuel?"

It turned out that Manuel's neighborhood was very familiar to Mrs. Wakefield, who, because of her interior design business, was familiar with most areas of the community. Soon she and Manuel were chatting like old friends. Manuel couldn't help thinking how nice it was to be made to feel right at home. Mrs. Wakefield was a wonderful woman—warm, relaxed, easy to talk to.

He couldn't help wishing he was talking to Sandra's mother instead of Elizabeth's. Why was it so hard to convince Sandra that it was essential that she introduce him to her parents? He wondered if he would ever be treated so warmly at the Bacons' house or if Sandy's mother would ever smile at him the way Mrs. Wakefield did.

Seven

"There it is," Sandra said proudly, pointing to the gleaming white motorboat whose prow bore the name *Solar One*. "That's *Solar*. We had a motorboat when I was little, and I've always loved them. I was so excited when my parents gave me this one last year."

Sandra, Elizabeth, and Manuel were strolling down the pier toward the basin of Secca Lake, where small boats were docked. Brilliant late-afternoon sunshine illuminated the sparkling water, and Elizabeth felt her spirits soar. It would be so nice to be out on the water.

"Are you a water-skier, Liz?" Sandra asked. "Or should we just go for a ride?"

"Let's just take her out and ride around," Manuel said, leaning over to untie the tether.

"Go on, you two, hop in," he instructed. "I'll follow."

"There's a life jacket on the seat," Sandra told Elizabeth. "Why don't you put it on? There are two more stored under the seats for Manuel and me."

Manuel leaped deftly into the boat, pulling the tether after him, and they bobbed gently on the brilliant water. Sandra seemed like a different person in the boat, very relaxed and sure of herself, Elizabeth thought, watching with admiration as she pulled the cord on the motor, sending it sputtering to life.

"We're ready to roll!" she shouted over the roar of the motor. After slipping on a pair of dark glasses, she jumped into the driver's seat. Manuel and Elizabeth sat down side by side on the seats behind Sandra. Behind them the engine was humming loudly. Elizabeth sighed happily as she shot forward.

"Hey!" Manuel cried. "Sandy, this is great."

"It sure is," Elizabeth agreed. It was a perfect afternoon. Sandra handled the little boat like a pro, turning expertly around the curve of the lake, and Elizabeth could see soft foam scissoring behind them.

"Hey," Manuel called loudly, leaning forward so Sandra could hear him, "let's cut the engine and just float for a while!"

Sandra obligingly cut the motor and reached behind her to squeeze his hand. "It's beautiful out here, isn't it?" she said, turning and smiling deeply into his eyes. "Sort of puts everything in perspective. I always feel like everything makes sense again when I come out here."

"Me, too," Manuel said seriously, staring at her.

Elizabeth blushed slightly. "I knew I'd be the proverbial third wheel," she said, teasing them. "Sandy, didn't I tell you that you two would have more fun out here without me?"

Frowning Manuel looked from Elizabeth to Sandra and back to Elizabeth again. "You mean—" he began. Then he shook his head and turned slightly away from Sandra. He stared out at the water.

"Let's start her up again," Sandra said, jumping out of the driver's seat as if she wanted to change the subject—fast. "Manuel, do me a favor and hold the wheel while I get her going."

Manuel gave Elizabeth a long look as he took the steering wheel, and Elizabeth suddenly felt uncomfortable. What was going on? Had Manuel really wanted her to come? She concentrated hard on looking at the lake, feeling less and less certain that she was really welcome.

"Darn it," Sandra said. "There's something weird going on with the motor." She jerked the cord, and the engine made several loud, rasping sounds, then died. "I wonder if we're out of gas. Liz, are there gas tanks under the seat?"

"They're right here," Liz said, pointing to the two gas tanks. "Do you want them?"

Sandra checked the gas level. "No, there's enough gas." She jerked hard on the cord again, and the engine came to life. It made a loud rattling noise that Elizabeth found alarming.

"I don't like the way this sounds!" Sandra hollered to Manuel. "Liz, can you hand me that tool kit that's up front? I want to fiddle around with this. Sounds like there might be something jammed in here. I need a wrench."

Elizabeth passed Sandra the kit. "Do you need help?" she cried over the loud roaring. The engine was smoking a little, and she coughed from the fumes. "Are you sure it's safe to play around with the engine?"

"Yes," Sandra assured her. "I had this happen once before. You stay up in the bow with Manuel," she cried.

Elizabeth turned and crawled back to the front of the boat, then clambered into the seat beside Manuel. Her heart was beating wildly, and she just wanted to get back to shore. The sound of the engine was making her increasingly uneasy. Suddenly the boat began to jerk violently, and the steering wheel shook in Manuel's hands.

The next thing Elizabeth knew, there was an incredible explosion.

Flames burst up from the engine, and Elizabeth screamed as the force of the blast sent her up into the air. Then the icy water of Secca Lake closed around her.

When she opened her eyes, she saw Manuel swimming toward her. Desperately he was calling out Sandra's name. Elizabeth felt dazed and dizzy from the shock of the explosion, but she managed to look around and realized that Sandra wasn't anywhere in sight.

"Are you all right?" she asked Manuel, pushing wet strands of hair out of her eyes.

Manuel was treading water, and he looked anxiously around him. "Where's Sandy?" he gasped, starting to swim toward the boat.

Elizabeth's eyes widened with terror as she stared up at the prow of *Solar One*. The engine was in flames. Was Sandra still in the boat? Heart pounding, Elizabeth swam after Manuel.

"There's gasoline stowed under the seat," she cried. "Manuel, the whole boat could explode any second!"

They both noticed at the same moment that Sandra had been thrown forward into the bow, where she now lay as the flames leaped higher and higher.

"She's passed out," Manuel gasped, grabbing the sides of the boat and pulling himself up. His arm muscles bulged with the strain as he hoisted himself in. Elizabeth, still dazed, bobbed helplessly in the water. The flames seemed to be everywhere, and for a moment she lost sight of Manuel.

"I've got her!" he cried. He jumped backward into the water, Sandra's limp form in his arms. "We've got to get out of here before that thing blows to bits," he gasped, holding Sandra's head up above water.

"Manuel," Elizabeth sobbed, "is she all right?"

"I don't know," Manuel choked out. He was swimming with one arm and holding Sandra up with the other, his wet clothes plastered to his body. "Do me a favor. Take off your life vest and let me put it on her. Are you strong enough to swim to shore?"

Elizabeth nodded, her fingers tearing at the belt of the vest. It took an agonizing minute to get it off, but finally she freed it and helped Manuel fasten it around Sandra.

"Manuel, what are we going to do?" Elizabeth asked as she treaded water.

"I want you to swim in front of me," Manuel gasped. "Just keep swimming. If you get tired, don't stop. Count under your breath. And remember, I'll be right behind you with Sandy. If you need to stop, I'll be there."

Tears of fear and frustration pricking her eyes, Elizabeth began to swim. The shoreline seemed incredibly far away, though she knew it couldn't be more than a quarter of a mile. Manuel was right behind her, his arm crooked around Sandra's chest.

Let her be all right, Elizabeth was thinking. *Just let her be all right.*

The next thing she knew, an incredible noise seemed to surround them. *Solar One* had exploded, and millions of tiny fiberglass fragments rained through the air. They had swum away just in time.

"Keep swimming," Manuel gasped. "We're almost there."

It seemed like ages before Elizabeth felt the bottom of the lake under her feet and she was able to stagger toward the beach. Manuel bent down then and picked Sandra up in his arms, then carried her the rest of the way. "She's coming to," he called to Elizabeth, his voice breaking with emotion. "She's got some bad burns on her hands, but she's coming to!"

Elizabeth crawled up onto the grassy edge of the lake and collapsed for a minute, trying to get her bearings. She saw a crowd of people over at the boathouse pointing toward them and guessed that their accident had been witnessed. That meant help would be coming.

Manuel lay Sandra down on the grass as if she were incredibly fragile. The girl was barely conscious. She was breathing irregularly and with a slight rasping sound. The palms of her hands were badly burned, and every now and then she moaned.

"It's OK, Sandy. I'm here," Manuel whispered, leaning over and wiping her face so tenderly that Elizabeth thought she was going to cry.

She couldn't believe what spectacular bravery she had just witnessed. Manuel had climbed into that boat knowing that it might explode at any instant; he had risked his own life, without a second's thought, to save Sandra.

And now, as he leaned over her, there was a combination of love, compassion, worry, and tenderness in his expression, such as Elizabeth had never seen before.

Eight

"Lie still," Manuel whispered soothingly to Sandra, smoothing her hair away from her forehead. "You're going to be all right, Sandy. You're going to be just fine."

Elizabeth looked with consternation at the crowd hurrying toward them. "I wish they'd hurry and get help," she said to Manuel.

Just then Sandra's eyes fluttered open. "Manuel," she said thickly. Her eyes closed again.

"Sandy!" Manuel cried, overwhelmed with joy that she was conscious. "Don't try to move or talk or anything," he admonished her the next instant. "Just lie still. Help is on the way."

"What happened?" she asked with difficulty, struggling to open her eyes again. "I was—I was at the back of the boat. There was this weird smell, and the engine . . ." She half sat up, an expression of terror on her face. "What happened to *Solar*? Where's the boat?"

"Sandy, you have to lie still," Manuel said softly, pushing her down very gently and looking at Elizabeth. "We need to cover her," he said anxiously. "I'm afraid she may go into shock."

"There was an explosion, wasn't there?" Sandra said, trying to sort out what had happened. Her eyes opened again, and she stared straight at Manuel. "You saved me, didn't you?" she murmured. "I was lying in the boat, and there were flames everywhere, and I thought I was going to die. And then I saw your face leaning over me, and I knew it was going to be all right. That was the last thing I remember."

"Shhh," Manuel whispered tenderly. "Don't tire yourself, Sandy. Look, people are coming with a stretcher. We're going to be able to move you to the boathouse and call an ambulance."

A grimace crossed Sandra's face as she lifted her hands. "My hands hurt, Manuel," she whispered.

"That's because they're burned," he whispered back, stroking her cheek. "Just lie still and try not to worry. Help is going to be here in just a second."

Sandra looked at Manuel with an expression of love so simple and passionate that again Elizabeth felt tears spring to her eyes. "Thank you," Sandra whispered, "for saving me."

Manuel leaned over her lovingly, not saying a word. Elizabeth got to her feet with effort, meaning to meet the rescuers who were hastening toward them with the stretcher.

"Is she all right?" one of the guards from the boathouse called.

"We need an ambulance!" Elizabeth called back. "She's badly burned."

"I'll run back to the boathouse and call for one," a young man said. The guard who had spoken had a blanket in his arms, and in the next minute Sandra and Manuel were surrounded by people, all asking questions and trying to help. Elizabeth crouched down to help tuck the woolen blanket around Sandra and saw the girl look up imploringly at Manuel.

"Listen," she whispered. "My parents . . . they don't know you came out with me this afternoon, Manuel." She closed her eyes and tears leaked out from behind her lids. "If they find out . . ."

Manuel gave her a look of agony. "What do you mean? I thought you were going to tell them."

She shook her head. "Please," she whispered. "Manuel, they mustn't find out. I told them it was just a friend . . . just Liz." She turned her imploring gaze to Elizabeth. "Will you back me up, Liz? If my parents find out Manuel was with us, I don't know what they'll do."

Elizabeth stared helplessly, first at Sandra, then at Manuel. "But—but Sandy, he saved your life," she stammered. In the confusion around them, no one really paid any attention to what they were saying.

"*You* saved me, Liz," she whispered thickly as two of the men lifted her onto the stretcher. Her eyes, shining with tears, fixed helplessly on Manuel as the men started to bear her away. "Forgive me," she whispered. And her eyelids dropped shut again, an expression of emotional and physical agony on her face as the men carried her away on the stretcher.

"Meet us at the boathouse," one of the guards called back to them. "The police are coming, and they're going to want to know what happened."

"I guess that's my cue to get lost," Manuel said bitterly, staring down at the ground. He looked, Elizabeth thought, positively exhausted. His face was streaked with sweat, and there was a long, jagged cut on his arm. Though he had no serious burns, his arms and face were singed, and he was obviously in pain.

"Manuel," Elizabeth said desperately. She wished there was something she could say or do to comfort him. But the truth was undeniable. Sandra wanted him gone, out of the picture. They both knew it.

"I'm out of here," Manuel said dully. And without another word he turned on his heel and trudged away, looking—Elizabeth thought —as if he had just lost his very best friend in the world.

By the time Elizabeth got to the boathouse, a chaotic scene greeted her eyes. The lifeguard was trying to organize everyone by calling out instructions through his megaphone, but the crowd of onlookers, boathouse staff, and park rangers were all getting in each other's way in their eagerness to help. Sandra was lying on the stretcher, still covered by a blanket, the park rangers had administered to her burns, and now she was waiting for the ambulance. She looked weak, but she was still conscious. Elizabeth pressed through the crowd and crouched down beside her.

"Sandy, are you all right?" she asked.

Sandra nodded. She was very pale, but otherwise she looked all right. "Has he gone?" she asked in a low voice.

Elizabeth swallowed. "Yeah. Sandy—"

"Don't say anything," Sandra pleaded. "I just couldn't bear it right now."

Elizabeth was quiet for a minute, listening to the frantic hubbub around them. Just then one of the park rangers approached them.

"My name is Don," he said, giving Sandra a concerned smile. "I work for the park service at Secca Lake. An ambulance is on its way and should be here in a few minutes. If you'll give me your phone number, we'll try to reach your parents so they can meet us at the hospital."

Sandra did as she was told, and Don wrote down the number.

"Now," Don said, looking businesslike and jotting notes on a pad of paper, "I need to ask you a couple of quick questions so I can file a report on the accident. How many of you were in the boat?"

"Just the two of us, Liz and me," Sandra said at once.

Elizabeth bit her lip and looked at the ground. *Poor Manuel*, she thought. This was all turning into a much bigger mess than she had feared.

"You must be Liz," Don said, turning to Elizabeth and giving her a smile. "You must be one extremely brave young lady. Did you really crawl back into the burning boat to rescue her?"

Elizabeth looked helplessly at Sandra. "I . . . uh . . ."

"Liz is incredibly modest. She'll never admit what she did," Sandra said. She looked imploringly at Elizabeth. "Come on, admit it. You saved my life."

Elizabeth looked around in horror as she saw a reporter from *The Sweet Valley News* bearing down on them. When had he arrived on the scene? How was she going to get out of this mess? Sandra was going to insist that Elizabeth was the one who had saved her, and the police *and* the reporter were going to believe her. It was bad enough to be given credit for something she hadn't done, especially when she knew how hurt Manuel had been when Sandra rejected him. But to lie, to tell the reporter that *she* had saved Sandra when in fact all she'd done was witness Manuel's heroics . . . Elizabeth had no idea what to do. Everything she stood for and believed in warned her against perpetuating Sandra's lie. But she had promised she wouldn't let anyone know that Manuel had been there with them. How could she betray Sandra in public without getting her into terrible trouble?

"I'll tell you how it happened," Sandra said weakly. "I was fixing the motor while Elizabeth steered the boat. I guess something was wrong with the engine, and it exploded. The impact was terrific, and Elizabeth got thrown into the water. I must've been knocked out at first because all I remember is looking up to see her crawling toward me through the flames." Sandra paused briefly, not meeting Elizabeth's eyes. "She was amazing. She didn't even stop to think that the boat was burning, that there was gas in the back, and that the whole thing could explode at any second. She got me in the water, took her own lifejacket off, and put it around me. Then she swam back to shore with me in her arms." This description had clearly exhausted Sandra, and she closed her eyes.

The reporter hovered around Elizabeth, demanding all sorts of information. He wanted to know her name, how long she had known Sandra, and what had gone through her mind when she saw the burning boat. Had she feared for her own life, or had her thoughts only been for Sandra?

One of the witnesses seemed uneasy about Sandra's story. "There were three of you, though," the blond boy who had run back to call the ambulance protested. He turned to Don. "I was on the dock with my friend Bert when we saw this huge burst of flames out in the middle of the lake. That's when we started calling for help. We didn't see anything for a long time. Then we saw people swimming. There were three of them, two girls and a guy. A muscular guy with dark, curly hair. And he was with you on the bank," he added stubbornly.

Sandra shook her head. "No," she said weakly. "It was just Liz."

"Look, son, she's tired," Don said to the boy. "I think we should let her rest until the ambulance comes."

But there was no need to wait any longer. The ambulance, its red light spinning and siren blaring, pulled up outside the boathouse. As the attendants from the ambulance hurried toward Sandra, Elizabeth had an overwhelming sense that she ought to say something to someone. She shouldn't be taking credit for something she hadn't done.

"Sandy," she said desperately as the girl was lifted up on the stretcher and carried toward the door.

"Don't worry," Sandra said weakly, her eyes pleading with Liz just before she was placed in the back of the ambulance. Elizabeth stared after her, completely at a loss. Now what was she supposed to do?

"Tell us exactly how it happened," the reporter demanded, his pencil poised above a pad of yellow paper. "I want to know exactly how you were able to save Sandra's life."

Elizabeth tried to get her bearings. "I—I'm sorry, but I'm really tired," she said, trying to stall for time. "I'm afraid I'm just not thinking very clearly. Could we talk about this later?"

"Just give us a brief description," the reporter begged. Behind him the photographer from the paper was positioning his camera, trying to get a good angle on Elizabeth.

"Well, it's exactly like Sandy said. She was trying to fix the engine, and there was an explosion," Elizabeth said. "That's really all I can remember clearly. I guess I was kind of shaken up from the explosion."

"So you managed to swim back to the boat and pull her out of the flames?" the reporter asked, scribbling furiously.

"I—yes, I guess that's what happened," Elizabeth said weakly.

She felt terrible. She couldn't remember ever having told such a blatant lie before. And the way they were all looking at her, with such admiration!

"Miss Wakefield, are you always this modest?" the reporter asked curiously. "This story is absolutely amazing. You saved someone's life, yet you don't seem to realize the extent of your bravery!"

97

Elizabeth blinked. "I'm not brave," she told him. That sounded strange, but she wasn't sure how to amend it without blurting out the whole truth and getting Sandra in trouble. "It just kind of happened," she added lamely. "Anyone would've done the same thing."

"Well, I don't think Sandy sees it that way," the reporter said. "And I don't think our readers are going to see it that way once we write up our story."

Elizabeth flushed. "Isn't there some way . . . I mean, do you *have* to write this up? I really feel uncomfortable about it. At least don't use my name," she begged.

"Elizabeth," the reporter said, shaking his head, "this isn't a misdemeanor we're writing about. It's an act of unbelievable courage. You have nothing to be ashamed of."

That's what you think, Elizabeth said to herself. She felt a knot forming in her stomach. What an incredible mess. Once the story ran in the paper, she was never going to hear the end of this. But she couldn't see a way out. If she told the reporter the truth—that Manuel had saved Sandra and she herself had been merely a spectator—the Bacons would find out that Sandra had been lying to them. They would find out about Manuel.

Sandra had put her in an incredibly awkward

position. Her choice was either to cover for her, which meant lying and taking credit for a heroic act she hadn't performed, or tell the truth and get her friend in trouble.

The cameraman snapped her picture, and Elizabeth tried her hardest to manage a shaky smile. She was absolutely dreading the moment when she saw her own image on the front page of the *News* the next morning!

Nine

"Liz," Jessica called, cupping her hand over the phone. "It's the head of the PTA! She wants to congratulate you on saving Sandy's life."

Elizabeth groaned. It was Wednesday morning, and the telephone had been ringing off the hook since the morning edition of *The Sweet Valley News* revealed the story about Elizabeth's incredible heroism. "Local Girl Saves Friend in Boating Accident" the headline ran, with a large picture of Elizabeth looking dazed and a little sheepish.

Elizabeth took the phone with a sigh. Mrs. Abernathy, the president of the Sweet Valley PTA, said cheerfully, "I'm sure that I'm the dozenth person to call this morning, but I just couldn't believe my eyes when I saw the paper this morning. I'm terrifically proud to have such

100

an outstanding young woman as a member of our school and our community."

"Thank you," Elizabeth said, "but I—"

Mrs. Abernathy cut her off. "You've set a remarkable example for other young people, Elizabeth. You demonstrated terrific courage and strength of mind in the face of a very difficult situation. I'm going to talk to Mr. Cooper about this, young lady. I think you should be given an award by the school board."

Mr. Cooper was the principal of Sweet Valley High. The thought of being given an award made Elizabeth cringe. In fact, she could hardly wait to get off the phone with Mrs. Abernathy, and she felt vastly relieved when, after a flurry of congratulations and unwarranted praise, the woman finally hung up.

"My sister, the hero," Jessica said with a smirk, buttering a piece of toast. Elizabeth had told the real story to her family, to Enid, and to Jeffrey, unable to keep up the preposterous lie in front of the people she was closest to. But everyone else believed what they read in the paper.

"I'm going straight over to Sandy's house after school this afternoon," she told Jessica with determination, "and I'm going to tell her that this can't go on. I mean, this is ridiculous! I don't want Mr. Cooper giving me an award for something I didn't even do! And think how horrible poor Manuel must feel," she added.

Jessica shrugged, her mouth full of toast. "Big deal," she mumbled. "I think it's great, Liz. If I were you, I'd milk this thing for all it's worth. Maybe they'll give you money instead of an award," she added thoughtfully.

"Jessica," Elizabeth said reproachfully, "don't you have the tiniest little sense of right and wrong?"

Jessica reached for another piece of toast. "Not in this case," she said cheerfully. "You're only going to mess things up if you start worrying about the truth *now*."

"Seems like your sister is giving you 'sound' advice, as always," Mr. Wakefield said, coming into the kitchen and giving each of his twin daughters a quick hug. "Don't let her fool you, Liz. There *is* something to be said for honesty, however complicated it makes your life."

"I'm calling Sandy," Elizabeth declared.

Sandra had been released from Fowler Memorial Hospital late Tuesday evening. She had been told to stay home from school for at least a couple of days, as she had second-degree burns on both palms and was still very shaken from the whole experience. Elizabeth was determined to see her first chance she got so they could figure out some sort of strategy. The thought of going to school and being treated like a hero was making her more and more uncomfortable—

especially when she imagined running into Manuel.

"Elizabeth!" Mrs. Bacon exclaimed when she called the Bacons' number. "Honey, we've just been talking about you. Every time I think of what you must have gone through yesterday, you two poor things . . . I'm telling you, I was up *all* night with the most dreadful dreams."

"How's Sandy?" Elizabeth asked weakly. She could understand the girl's position a little better whenever she had to confront Mrs. Bacon. She was a very overbearing woman.

"Well, she's all right, thank heavens. Thanks to *you*." Mrs. Bacon said vehemently. "Good gracious, Elizabeth. Sandy's father and I have been talking about *nothing else* since this happened. And we've both agreed that under the circumstances we want to do something special for you. Something to let you know how much we appreciate what you did for Sandy."

"That's totally unnecessary," Elizabeth said quickly, alarmed.

"Nonsense!" Mrs. Bacon said. "Just a little something," she added mysteriously. "Nothing we can give you could possibly be equal to your heroism." She was quiet for a minute, and Elizabeth had the sense she was running through some kind of grim imaginary scenario. "When I *think* of that poor child lying in that burning boat . . ."

"Well," Elizabeth said doubtfully, "maybe we should all try to forget about it. I just wanted to see how Sandy was feeling this morning, and I was wondering if I could stop by to see her this afternoon after school.

"I'm sure she would love that," Mrs. Bacon said immediately.

Elizabeth was thoughtful for a minute after she had hung up the phone.

"Come on," Jessica said impatiently. "We're going to be late for school. And I don't want to ruin your grand entrance!"

Elizabeth gave her a dirty look. "You know," she said after a pause, "it's a funny thing about Mrs. Bacon. You'd think she'd realize that Sandy is too old to hang on to so tightly. It seems as if she thinks she can tell exactly what her daughter is thinking and feeling all the time. As though there's no difference between her daughter's life and her own."

Jessica snorted. "We should introduce her to Manuel. That ought to prove to her how wrong she is."

"Actually," Elizabeth said slowly, "I think you happen to be right, Jess. I think Sandy needs to break away from her parents a little bit. And I think Manuel has gotten himself caught right in the middle."

*   *   *

104

By the time Elizabeth got to Sandra's house that afternoon, she was exhausted and extremely upset. The school day had seemed interminable. Manuel had been absent, which meant she couldn't even talk to him about what had happened. Because Sandra was absent too, Elizabeth was the one everyone accosted for information about the accident. She thought if she heard one more hearty "Congratulations!" or "Liz, you were so brave!" she would die. Jeffrey actually saved her sanity by taking her out for lunch off-campus, so she was spared interrogation during that hour at least. By four o'clock, when she arrived at the Bacons' house, she was more determined than ever that Sandra would have to tell the truth.

But before she got to see Sandra, she had to deal with Mrs. Bacon.

"Sandy's father will be so upset that he missed you. But this is from both of us," Mrs. Bacon said, pressing a small box into Elizabeth's hand.

Elizabeth looked at it with alarm. "But—I really don't want you to give me anything," she protested.

"Just open it!" Mrs. Bacon commanded, beaming.

Elizabeth sighed and obediently opened the small box. Her heart fell as she saw the beautiful, rope-link gold bracelet inside. It was from

Stowe's, the nicest jewelry store in Sweet Valley, and obviously had cost a lot of money.

"Honestly, Mrs. Bacon, I can't accept something like this," Elizabeth protested.

But Mrs. Bacon would hear none of it. "Let me put it on for you," she said with a cheerful, no-nonsense air that was impossible to object to. Elizabeth had to admit the bracelet was gorgeous, and she thanked Mrs. Bacon with as much enthusiasm as she could muster. She could hardly wait to get upstairs and confront Sandra—alone.

"Sandy," she said, closing her friend's bedroom door firmly behind her, "we have *got* to do something! This is a catastrophe!"

Sandra, wearing a pretty ruffled nightgown, was sitting up in bed. She looked absolutely fine, and except for the white bandages on her hands Elizabeth would never have known she had been through such a terrible ordeal. "What do you mean?" Sandra asked. "Have you seen Manuel? Is he mad at me? Was he in school? I've tried calling him, but there's been no one at home at his house all day."

"He wasn't in school," Elizabeth said. "But, Sandy, that isn't the point." She showed Sandra the bracelet on her wrist. "This is! Do you realize that people are treating me like a hero? All I've heard for the past twenty-four hours is how brave I am, how wonderful and courageous I was to save you. Poor Manuel must feel awful!"

Sandra looked distressed. "I know. I'll have to try to explain it all to him somehow. But, Liz, there's nothing we can do now. You don't mind that much, do you? I mean, can you put up with it for just a few more days until all the fuss dies down?"

Elizabeth sat down on the side of the bed. "Look, Sandy, I want to help you out. But the truth is that I'm not a good liar. I feel rotten letting people think I've done something that I haven't. And accepting an expensive present like this from your parents . . ."

"Oh, that," Sandra said disparagingly. "Don't worry about *that*. Liz, please keep the bracelet. You don't have to wear it if it makes you feel funny. But do me a favor and keep it. Don't blow my cover!" Tears formed in her eyes. "I'm afraid that if my parents found out the truth, they'd never forgive me."

"But why?" Elizabeth cried. "The truth is that *Manuel* saved you, not me. Wouldn't your parents realize what a fine person he is if they knew that?"

"They can't help the way they are," Sandra said stubbornly. "All they would see when they looked at Manuel is that he's Mexican. They have blinders on."

"Well, I can't interfere with you and your parents. But I think you're making a mistake," Elizabeth said. "I think you're afraid of them, Sandy. And sooner or later you're going to have to take a stand. Especially if you really love Manuel, you're going to have to be willing to fight for him." She got to her feet.

"Liz," Sandra said in a choked voice, "will you do me one more favor? Will you go over to Manuel's house and tell him I love him and that I'm sorry?"

Elizabeth looked down at the girl with compassion. "All right," she said softly.

Her heart went out to Sandra. It was obvious how tortured she felt. And it was clear that unless she was able to stand up to her parents and admit her true feelings soon, she was going to crack. No one could lead a double life for long, not even someone as resolute as Sandra Bacon.

Elizabeth stopped by the Lopezes' house on her way home. She was more than a little anxious about seeing Manuel, who she assumed would be livid. *Oh, well*, she said philosophically to herself. *I guess I'm in this whole mess so far by now, I might as well go ahead and see if I can't try to make Manuel feel better.* But she wasn't all that hopeful as she rang the door bell.

Manuel answered the door after several minutes. "Liz!" he said, looking surprised. "Come in."

Elizabeth had never been to his house before, and she noticed with admiration the casual warmth of the decor. "My mom is out with my brothers and sister," Manuel explained, taking Elizabeth back to the porch. "I know they'll be sorry to have missed you." His voice was polite but strained, and Elizabeth was aware that he was holding back great emotion.

"Look, Manuel, let's level with each other. What happened yesterday was absolutely rotten," Elizabeth said. "I know how hurt you must be."

Manuel leaned forward intently. "Have you seen Sandy?" Is she OK? I called the hospital, and they said she'd been released, but it's killing me, not knowing how she *really* is. Is she—?" His voice faltered. "Did she ask about me?" He sighed. "I couldn't bear to go to school today and answer questions. I can't believe I did it, but I faked an excuse. I called in, pretending to be my father, and said I was sick." He shook his head. "So tell me about her. You've seen her?"

Elizabeth nodded. "She asked me to come here to see you. She wanted me to tell you—" Elizabeth broke off. "That she's sorry," she said at last.

Manuel's face lit up. "As long as she's all right," he said happily.

Elizabeth stared at him. "You're not going to accept her apology, are you? Aren't you sick of her trying to hide you?"

Manuel looked down at his hands. "To be honest with you, Liz, I just don't know what to do anymore. It's like losing the needle on the compass. I have no idea any more which way to go." He sighed heavily. "Yes, it hurts. What happened yesterday"—his expression darkened—"that hurt pretty bad." He looked down at his hands. "I've seen all the papers. I know you must feel really weird having to go along with Sandy's lie. But, Liz, she can't help it!" he cried. "I want so much to believe that, anyway," he added feelingly.

Elizabeth couldn't believe her ears. The last thing on earth she would have expected was that Manuel would be defending Sandra to her.

Her hunch was that it wouldn't last. But then how was anyone to tell?

Ten

Sandra had been counting the minutes until Friday morning, when she was allowed to go back to school. It seemed like an eternity since the boating accident and since she had seen Manuel. They had only spoken on the phone two times, and both conversations had been brief—and anxiety-ridden on her part. She was constantly afraid her mother would pick up the phone and ask who she was talking to. It was also hard to tell on the phone how Manuel was feeling. She guessed his feelings were hurt by her behavior, but from what Elizabeth had told her about her talk with him on Wednesday, she was confident he'd be willing to give her another chance.

It took her a long time to get dressed that morning, because of the bandages on her hands, but still she dressed with special care, deliberately wearing blue, Manuel's favorite color on her. Because of the bandages, she couldn't drive to school, which meant her mother had to take her, and she was too late to catch Manuel before first-period class. In fact, she didn't see Manuel the entire morning. At last she caught up to him in the corridor right before lunch. "Manuel!" she called. "I've been looking for you everywhere!"

Manuel turned, his dark eyes grave. He glanced briefly down at the bandages on her hands. "Are you OK? I didn't think you'd be back to school so soon," he said quietly.

Sandra shrugged. "My hands still hurt, but it's no big deal. But it's you I've been worrying about. Elizabeth said—" She faltered. "Elizabeth thought you weren't that mad at me about what happened on Tuesday. I mean—"

Manuel stared down at the ground. "I guess I've just had to face the fact that you don't really care enough about me to be seen with me in public. I've thought a lot about us this week, Sandy. I don't want to have to say this, but I think what you did was unfair. At first all I cared about was hearing whether or not you were all right. But after Elizabeth left. . . ." He stared helplessly at her. "I just can't go on like this, Sandy. I understand you're afraid to talk to your parents, but it isn't right. If you really loved me, you'd confront them."

Sandra's eyes filled with tears. "That isn't true. It's just that I need more time!"

"Yeah," Manuel said, a trace of bitterness in his voice. "That's what you've been saying for weeks, Sandy. I don't think you're being honest with yourself. I don't think you're ever going to be ready to confront them."

Sandra grabbed his arm. "What are you saying?" she cried, panic-stricken. "Are you trying to tell me that you want to break up?"

"It isn't up to me," Manuel said sadly. "What I want is for you to be my girlfriend. I want us to be able to go places together. I want to meet your parents and be able to pick you up at your house when we have a date. I'm sick of sneaking around like some kind of criminal. Sandy, I love you, but I need to feel you respect me. Enough to confront your parents. Enough to tell everyone we're going out instead of hiding it!"

Sandra swallowed; her throat ached. "Can't you give me just a little more time?" she pleaded.

Manuel frowned. "I've waited, Sandy. I've been patient. Now it's your turn." And with that he turned and walked away, leaving her staring after him. Tears streamed down her cheeks. The worst thing was that she knew he was right.

The time had come to make a choice. She only hoped she wasn't too late. She may already have lost Manuel's love forever.

"Manuel?" Pete Young said, coming into the track office where Manuel was working that afternoon. "There are a couple of men here who want to talk to you about that boating accident on Tuesday. You don't mind answering a question or two for them, do you?"

Manuel raised his eyebrows. "Not at all. Who are they?"

Pete, the coach at the elementary school, looked apprehensively at the door. "Police," he said. "Manuel, they look real serious. You've got nothing to hide, do you?"

Manuel bit his lip. "Nope," he said, shoving his hands in his pockets.

The door opened, and two policemen came in. Their expressions were serious, but Manuel couldn't imagine what they would have to ask him about.

"Are you Manuel Lopez?" the first officer asked, showing Manuel his identification card. His name was Richard Patterson.

Manuel nodded.

"I'm Officer Patterson, and this is Sergeant James. We want to ask you a few questions

114

about the boat accident that took place at Secca Lake Tuesday. Do you know anything about it?"

Manuel shook his head. "Not really. I mean, I saw it happen and everything. I was on the shore when the two girls came back. I tried to help Sandy. That's all." The words stuck in his throat. He couldn't believe this was happening.

"Well," Officer Patterson said, looking at a pad of paper he had withdrawn from his breast pocket, "we've got some witnesses who claim they saw you hanging around the boat just before the girls got in. Can you tell me a little more precisely what you were doing down by the dock before the girls left?"

Manuel reddened. "Are you suggesting that I did something wrong?"

Sergeant James raised his eyebrows. "We never said anything about doing something wrong. What makes you mention that, son? Have you got something on your mind?"

This was unbelievable. It was bad enough he hadn't been given the credit for saving Sandra's life, but now they were actually going to accuse him of tampering with the boat. He felt his face get hot and red. He didn't think he was going to be able to control his temper a minute longer. His heart was pounding, and he was furious.

"Listen," he said. "I'm a friend of Sandy's,

all right? I was helping her get the boat into the water. That's all." He was sure Sandra wouldn't mind if he said that. The Bacons couldn't possibly object to their daughter receiving assistance from a friend, even a Mexican friend! "That's all there is to it."

"Fine," Officer Patterson said, snapping his pad closed. He gave Sergeant James a look that seemed to suggest that there was more to the whole thing as far as *they* were concerned.

"I think you'd better come down to the station to fill out a few forms for us. Just as a witness," Sergeant James added.

Manuel was stunned. He didn't like their tone one bit. It was one thing not to receive credit for having saved Sandra's life. Manuel didn't even mind that; he didn't care about being a hero. He had saved Sandra because he loved her with all his heart, and anything else would have been unfathomable.

But he didn't like being accused of a crime. And if anyone thought they were going to blame him in some way for what had gone wrong with the boat, they had another thought coming.

"I don't understand what's going on," Sandra said to her mother. After watching cheerleading practice, her mother had been waiting for her outside in the Toyota. "We're meeting your father at the police station," Mrs. Bacon said, her face pale. "They think there may have been foul play involved in your accident, honey. Apparently there's some suspicion that someone might have tampered with the motor before you left the dock. And they have a suspect."

Sandra stared at her. "Who would do something like that?" she demanded.

"That's exactly what they intend to find out. Don't worry about it now, dear," her mother said soothingly. "Your father and I will be there with you the whole time. And if they ask anything you don't want to answer, or try to put you on the spot, we'll call an end to the whole thing at once."

Sandra regarded her mother. "Mom, whose idea was it to investigate the accident—yours, or theirs?"

Mrs. Bacon frowned. "Well, of course it was theirs, dear. It's just a routine investigation. Although it's true that your father and I made a point of letting them know that if there *had* been foul play, we certainly wanted whoever was responsible to be properly punished."

Sandra had a queasy feeling in her stomach. Something told her that her parents were pushing the police, that they *wanted* there to have been foul play. It was typical, she thought. Her

117

parents always wanted to find a scapegoat. They couldn't believe that things just went wrong by themselves sometimes.

Mr. Bacon was waiting for them at the police station. "Don't be nervous, honey," he said to Sandra. "Your mother and I are going to be here the whole time."

"I just don't understand what's going on. There wasn't any foul play. The motor blew up," Sandra said, upset.

"Shhh, dear. Just let your father and me handle this," her mother admonished her. Officer Patterson and Sergeant James were waiting for them inside the station, and soon they were all seated on uncomfortable chairs in Sergeant James's office.

"Well," the sergeant said slowly, "it looks like you two were right. We do have reason to suspect that there may have been someone tampering with the engine. We have reports from several witnesses that a young Mexican boy was seen out by the dock talking to Elizabeth and Sandy before they left. Apparently he was seen looking at the boat before they got in."

"Sandy, is this true? You never said anything to us about it," Mrs. Bacon said, distressed.

Sandra stared at the policeman. She couldn't believe it. Manuel? They suspected *Manuel* of tampering with the engine?

"We've got the young man in question right here," Sergeant James went on. "He claims that he's a close friend of your daughter's, that they know each other well, and that all he was doing was helping her."

"Sandy!" Mrs. Bacon exclaimed, her face turning red. "Why, that's nonsense," she declared. "My daughter doesn't associate with that sort of person."

"What sort of person, Mrs. Bacon?" Officer Patterson asked.

Sandra felt the blood pounding in her head. She couldn't believe this was happening.

"Sandy," her father said in a low voice, "tell us the truth. You don't have any friends who we haven't met, do you? We've always trusted you. Your mother and I will believe whatever you tell us."

Sandra opened her mouth, but no words came out. She was close to tears. She wanted to tell them the truth—but she couldn't do it. With a kind of dazed horror, she heard herself saying something completely untrue.

"I don't know what you're talking about," she said to the policeman. "I don't remember talking to anyone. He must be lying. He's not a friend of mine."

"I knew there must be a mistake," Mrs. Bacon said, relieved.

"Manuel? Come in here." Sergeant James said, opening the door and gesturing at Manuel, who had been waiting outside in the hallway. "The girl says she doesn't know you. This doesn't look good, I'm afraid. Have you been lying to us?"

Staring down at the ground, Manuel walked into the office. His face was expressionless.

Sandra felt dizzy. She couldn't believe Manuel was actually there and she was going to have to look him in the face and claim she didn't know him. But she had lied too much to back down now. And her parents' presence on either side of her was so strong . . .

"I'm going to ask you once more," Sergeant James said directly to Sandra. "Do you know this young man?"

"No," she said in a clear, strong voice. "I've never seen him before in my life."

Eleven

A long silence followed Sandra's declaration. Then Sergeant James cleared his throat. "We were afraid of this," he said, looking at Manuel. "We called Elizabeth Wakefield and asked her to come in to confirm what Sandra reports. But I'm afraid it doesn't look very good for you, Manuel. We've got several witnesses claiming they saw you poking around the boat before the girls left. You told us you were a friend of Miss Bacon's. Now she's saying she doesn't even know who you are. I'm afraid we're going to have to hold you here for a few hours while we ask you some more questions." He jerked his head at Mr. Bacon. "We won't trouble you any more, sir."

Manuel turned, then, and faced Sandra. As long as she lived, she would never forget the pain she felt when his eyes met hers. "Sandy," he said simply. "How could you?"

Sandra promptly burst into tears. "Mom," she said, gasping through her sobs, "Dad, I have something to tell you. I *do* know Manuel."

"Wait a minute," Sergeant James said. "What's going on? Sandy, we aren't playing games here. This is a very serious matter."

"Sandy, honey, I know you want to help this boy, but you don't have to lie on his behalf," Mrs. Bacon said, alarmed by her daughter's tears. "Calm down, sweetheart. You've been through a terrible shock, and clearly this boy is putting some kind of pressure on you." She looked angrily at Manuel. "Can't you see that she's upset? I think we ought to go home."

Sandra shook her head, trying to fight for control. "No, Mom. Listen to me. I've been lying, not just to the policemen, but to you and Dad as well. Manuel *is* my friend. More than my friend. He saved my life when the boat exploded. If it weren't for him—" She rubbed the tears from her eyes. "If it weren't for him, I'd be dead."

"But you told us Elizabeth saved you," Mr. Bacon said, confused. "Sandy, what's going on here? What are you trying to tell us?"

"I'm trying to tell you that I'm in love with Manuel," she cried. "I think it's too late now, because I've been horrible. I've lied, I've been ashamed, I've been too afraid to face you and tell you how I really feel. But the truth is, I love him. He saved my life, and I love him." At this point Sandra burst into hysterical tears again and crumbled up on the chair. She cried as if her heart were breaking, and Mr. and Mrs. Bacon stared at her as if she were a total stranger.

"Sandy, what are you saying?" Mrs. Bacon cried. "You mean to tell me that you—and *this* boy—"

Sandra could tell from her mother's expression exactly what was about to follow. Her mother was going to go through her litany of things wrong with Mexicans. She was going to humiliate Manuel in front of the policemen. But Sandra cut her off before she could say another word. Anger was building up inside her until she thought she might choke, and suddenly she knew she could do it. At last she found the courage to face her mother. In her agitation, she didn't notice that the office door had opened and Elizabeth Wakefield had slipped inside.

"Mother," she said in a forceful voice, "let me tell you exactly what I mean. All my life you and Daddy have tried to teach me that the most important values are honesty and respect for other people. Well, Manuel Lopez stands for those virtues more than any other boy I've ever met. He is loving, thoughtful, responsible, and more than all that, he's brave. For weeks he's wanted me to face you, to tell you that we'd fallen in love. But I was a coward." Sandra hung her head for a second, then looked intently first at her mother, then at her father. "It's hard for me to admit, but I was ashamed of you two," she said softly. "I was ashamed to admit that you could be prejudiced. It was the first time I had to face the fact that you two weren't always perfect."

Mrs. Bacon started to protest, but Mr. Bacon held her back. "She's right," he said softly. "Go on, Sandy. I think your mother and I both need to hear what you have to say."

She drew a long, quavering breath. "It's just that you've always taught me to be tolerant, to try to learn as much about the world as possible. When I met Manuel, I fell in love. He's just about the best thing that's ever happened to me." She still couldn't meet Manuel's gaze. "And I did something to him that is simply inexcusable. Manuel wanted to go out in the boat, not so much because of the boat itself, but because he thought it represented a new step. He thought I had told you about inviting him, that it meant I would be ready to introduce you to him. Instead I lied. I invited Liz Wakefield to come, too, as a kind of cover."

"Oh, Sandy," Mrs. Bacon said, distraught.

"Let me finish, Mom," Sandra begged. "So

the three of us went out. You know the rest of it. The engine developed trouble, and I tried to fix it. What you don't know is that Liz and Manuel were thrown into the water by the impact of the first explosion. *Manuel* was the one who swam back to the boat and saved me. Manuel was the one who risked his life to crawl through those flames." Sandra buried her face in her hands. "And how did I repay him? By asking him to get lost as soon as we were safe on shore so no one would know he'd been with us, so you wouldn't find out the truth."

Mrs. Bacon stared at Manuel in utter bewilderment. Then she turned to Elizabeth, who had been listening to Sandra's testimony with sympathetic admiration. "Liz, is this true? Is Sandy telling me the truth?" she asked wonderingly.

Elizabeth, her voice heavy with emotion, said, "Everything Sandy just said is absolutely true. I feel horrible having acted the part of a hero when I was just a witness. Manuel's the real hero, the one who really saved your daughter's life."

"But, Liz, you only acted the part because I forced you to," Sandra said loyally. "You were trying to be a good friend despite your better judgment."

Mr. Bacon got to his feet and looked hard at Manuel. "Young man," he said seriously, "I have a question for you."

"Yes, sir," Manuel said respectfully.

"As far as I can deduce from this convoluted tale my daughter is telling, you two fell in love. Am I right?"

Manuel nodded.

"And you wanted to meet us, to come out in the open about the whole thing, but Sandy insisted you keep things quiet. Right again?" Manuel nodded again. "OK. Now the day of the accident comes, and you, with unbelievable courage and devotion, jump back into the boat and save Sandy. You swam with her to shore. Why did you agree to leave? Why did you let the whole community think Liz had saved her?"

Manuel was quiet for a long moment. "Sir," he said at last, "I love Sandy. I wouldn't hurt her for the world. I believed what she was doing was wrong, but I knew she wasn't ready to face you yet. I had to keep quiet. I owed it to her."

Mr. Bacon shook his head, amazed. "And you would've let us believe you had actually tampered with the engine? You would've taken *blame* for an act when actually you deserved incredible acclaim?"

Here Manuel hesitated. "I think, sir, that I wouldn't have taken blame for something I didn't do. To keep quiet is one thing, but to confess to a crime, one I didn't commit, well. . . . My family is very proud, Mr. Bacon. I think it would break my parents' hearts if they thought I'd done something they couldn't be proud of."

Mr. Bacon looked long and hard at Manuel before clearing his throat. "You know," he said finally, "if you were my son, I'd be proud of you." He offered Manuel his hand to shake. "I want to thank you for saving my daughter's life. And I want you to know that you're always welcome in our home."

Mrs. Bacon looked miserable and confused, as if she didn't know what to do or say first. "I—I feel like I ought to thank you, too," she said uncertainly. She stared down at the floor. Lifetime prejudices were hard to shed in a moment, and it was evident that she was feeling distinctly uncomfortable about the idea of Manuel and Sandra as a couple. But it was also evident that she was trying very hard.

"I feel I owe my daughter thanks, too," she added looking at Sandra. "I don't know when you grew up as fast as you did, but suddenly you're not a child anymore. You're a young woman with your own opinions and feelings. Until this afternoon I don't think I realized how hard I was trying to hang on to you, how hard I was trying to keep you young. You've both taught me a lesson today."

"Oh, Mom," Sandra said, jumping up and throwing her arms around her mother.

"Well," Sergeant James said, clearing his throat, "this is probably the nicest resolution to suspected foul play we've seen around this station. Wouldn't you agree, Officer Patterson?"

Richard Patterson laughed. "I think you're right," he agreed cheerfully. "And I don't know about anyone else here, but I'm just about ready to call it a day."

Sandra released her mother, but she was almost afraid to turn around and meet Manuel's gaze.

"Hey," he said softly, touching her arm. "Any chance I can interrupt this and get a minute alone with you?"

"Go on," Mrs. Bacon said, dabbing at her eyes with a tissue. "You two go ahead." She smiled through her tears. "After what you've both been through, I think you deserve a chance to be alone together. Don't you think so, Bob?"

Mr. Bacon nodded. "You know, Manuel," he said suddenly, "the country club we belong to is having a big dance next week. We've been trying to twist Sandy's arm to get her to go, but she's refused up till now. Something tells me if you'd agree to come, she might just reconsider." He winked at Sandra. "What do you think? Think you could stand that stuffy old club if you had a buddy to keep you company?"

"I'd be very glad to come," Manuel told him,

"but only if your whole family will be my family's guests at the Mexican festival, which is also coming up next week."

"Manuel," Mr. Bacon said, leaning over to shake his hand, "you've got yourself a deal."

Sandra's eyes glistened. She didn't know whether to laugh or cry. All she knew was that everything was going to work out. It was like magic, and the most incredible thing of all was the look of tender forgiveness on Manuel's face as he took her hand and led her out of the office.

"God, I've missed you," Sandra said breathlessly, her arms around Manuel's neck as she stared up into his eyes. Manuel had given her a ride home from the police station, but they had stopped at Miller's Point, a scenic spot that was popular with Sweet Valley High students. Within seconds Sandra was in Manuel's arms.

"Me, too," Manuel said. "Sandy, those days without you were just unbearable. I didn't even know how you were, and the thought of not being able to visit you . . ."

"Let's never have another misunderstanding," Sandra whispered.

Manuel smoothed back her hair, his eyes concerned. "That sounds good, but we *will* have misunderstandings; couples always do. We just have to count on the fact that underneath it all we're friends. We'll get through somehow."

Sandra snuggled up to him. "I always want to remember this moment," she told him. She knew that Manuel was right. They *would* have misunderstandings again, but they would find a way to get through them.

She felt as if an incredible weight had been lifted from her shoulders. For the first time in her whole life, she had stood up to her parents and fought for something she believed in. And they backed her! She would never forget the warmth that had flooded through her when her father shook Manuel's hand.

"It's going to be a new beginning," she whispered, "for all of us."

"Yeah," Manuel said huskily. "Only we want to make sure to hang on to some of the great things from the past, too. Like this." And the next minute his lips were on hers, and she forgot everything, except how wonderful it was to be in love, and to know at last that she and Manuel had nothing to hide.

Twelve

"The question is," Cara said, looking around at the decorations festooning the Wakefields' living room, "how are we going to get Lila over here tonight? She won't even *speak* to any of us, and she's maddest at you, Jess. I really don't think she's going to agree to it."

"Cara's right," Amy Sutton chimed in. "I've never seen Lila in a mood like she was in yesterday. Boy," she said happily, "when we all ran into her at the mall and pretended we didn't even remember it was her birthday . . ."

"And then going on and on about the concert we all supposedly were going to," Jessica said gleefully. "She looked like she was about to murder us!"

"So how are we going to get her to just drop by?" Cara asked. "Jessica, Lila told me yesterday that she never wants to speak to you again as long as she lives."

Jessica seemed completely unperturbed. "Look, this is going to be simple," she replied. "Lila's feeling a little edgy today, which under the circumstances is understandable. So, you're right, she probably won't be up for coming over. At least not voluntarily."

Amy, who was in the middle of blowing up a big balloon that said "Happy Birthday Lila" on it, gave Jessica a look. "You can't possibly be thinking what I think you're thinking," she said suspiciously.

"Here's your mission, you two," Jessica said with a grin, looking from Cara to Amy. "At seven-thirty you go over to Lila's house to apologize. Tell her you want to take her out for an ice cream and to help her plan her revenge on me. She ought to agree to *that*. You have to lay it on really thick so she thinks you've really rethought the whole thing and are feeling rotten. Then, once you get her in the car, you drive her over here. If she protests, tell her you want her to confront me, that you want us to hash it out. When she gets here, the whole house will be dark and quiet. You ring the door bell to warn us, and we all jump out and yell 'Surprise!' And Lila will practically fall over, she'll be so shocked."

"Jess, you're a genius," Amy declared.

"I have to hand it to you. It does sound pretty good," Cara agreed. "And this place looks wonderful!"

Jessica looked around with a pleased smile. The "Surprise Surprise Party" banner, which Jeffrey and Elizabeth had made, was stretched across one end of the living room, and Jessica and Cara's "This Is Your Life, Lila Fowler" banner was stretched across the other. Balloons were everywhere, and Jessica had set up card tables covered with bright tablecloths for the spread she and Cara were preparing. They had tons of ice cream in Lila's favorite flavor, million-dollar mocha, and four luscious chocolate cakes shaped as letters that spelled out her name.

Jessica knew it was going to be a wonderful party. She just couldn't wait to see the look on Lila's face when she walked through the door and everyone jumped out from behind the furniture yelling "Surprise!"

"I don't care what you two say," Lila said crossly, shaking free of Amy's grasp as Amy and Cara half coaxed, half dragged the resistant girl up the front steps of the Wakefields' house. "I absolutely refuse to speak to her. If you drag me in there, I'll just stand there and stare at her. I'm not going to say one single word."

Cara winked at Amy. "Well, as long as you come inside and just listen. Honestly, Lila, you two are going to have to make up sometime."

"Over my dead body!" Lila snapped. "I sort of forgive you two, though not completely," she added quickly. "But I know it was Jessica who put you up to it. That girl," she fumed. "After all the things I've done for her, after all the times I've helped her plan parties over at my place . . ."

Amy leaned over and rang the door bell. "Well, just take it easy," she advised. "You never know, Lila. You might just regret being so hard on her."

"Never!" Lila declared. "And if you think I'm going to back down and talk to her, you're insane!"

"Let's go in. The door's open," Amy said, stepping aside so Lila could go in first.

Lila looked suspiciously into the darkened front hallway. "It's probably rigged," she muttered. "Jessica's probably got a bomb set to go off as soon as I walk in." She tossed her head imperiously. "All right. I'll just march right in and tell her exactly what I think of her!"

Amy and Cara had to cover their mouths to keep from laughing out loud. The minute Lila crossed the threshold, lights snapped on all over the house, and the air filled with shouts of "Surprise!"

Lila was so astonished she literally swayed as if she were going to fall down. "Oh, no!" she cried, clapping her hand over her mouth. "I'm not even dressed up. I look like a total jerk!" She gazed with complete disbelief at the decorations, the banners, the group of animated friends, who were all chanting her name. And in front of them all was Jessica, whose face was absolutely radiant.

"Jessica," Lila stammered, dazed. "Jessica, how—I mean, what—I thought—"

"You thought we all forgot you. But we just wanted this to be a *real* surprise," Jessica said happily. The next minute Lila was surrounded by dozens of her classmates, each trying to crowd in to give her a hug or hand her a present.

"Jess, I've got to hand it to you," Lila said, wiping her eyes. "You really surprised me. In fact, you shocked me. Yesterday I thought I didn't have a friend in the world. And today I feel—well, I just feel amazingly happy." She looked around at her friends and smiled. "I feel like the luckiest person in the world."

"What do you think?" Jessica demanded, hurrying up to her twin several minutes after the party had really gotten under way. Loud music was booming from the stereo, and the dancing had gotten so energetic that Jessica had shooed people out onto the deck. About thirty of the twins' classmates had shown up, and everyone seemed to be having a fantastic time.

"Well, Lila looks as though she's forgiven you," Elizabeth said, pointing to the corner where Lila was intent on opening the first present from the stack she had been given. "Something tells me she's going to forget all about how cruelly you treated her."

"I don't suppose," a low voice said with a mock-growl behind them, "that I can grab the older of you two clones for a quick dance?"

Elizabeth's eyes brightened. "Jeffrey," she said huskily, stepping into his arms with a smile.

Jessica rolled her eyes and hurried off to find Amy and Cara. Her mood was too good to be spoiled just because her serious sister had tied herself down to Jeffrey French.

Lila's birthday party was a roaring success. And all the credit was going exactly where it was deserved—to Jessica herself. She couldn't remember when she had had such a good time!

"Don't tell me you're leaving already!" Elizabeth cried, hurrying after Enid as her friend, jacket draped over her arm, headed out to the Wakefields' foyer.

"It was a great party, Liz. You'll have to thank Jessica for me again. But I promised my mom I'd be home early." Enid's eyes shone. "You know how many zillions of little last-minute things there are to do before someone comes for a visit." Her face was flushed with anticipation. "Only Nana isn't just coming for a visit. She's moving in. Really and truly moving in!"

Enid had just learned that very day that all the efforts she and her mother had put into convincing her grandmother to move out to California had succeeded. Her grandmother would be arriving the very next week! Now suddenly it seemed there was not much time left, and so much to do. Enid's grandmother had aged considerably since her last visit, and Enid and her mother were going to have to work hard to make the house comfortable for her. They had decided that Enid's bedroom would be the best place for Nana to stay, and Enid was going to move up to the attic.

"Promise you'll let me help you," Elizabeth begged her. "I know you're going to have a lot of work to do."

Enid's eyes were very bright. "Who cares about the work?" she said cheerfully. "The important thing is that Nana is moving in. She won't be lonesome anymore. And we'll be a real family!"

Elizabeth knew how important the notion of

family was to Enid. Her parents were divorced, and she was the only child, so she had a real sense of how much her mother depended on her, and vice versa. Elizabeth couldn't help wonder, though, what new pressures would be exerted on Enid now that her grandmother would be living with them.

She gave her friend an impulsive hug. "Well, I'm sorry you have to leave early, but I know it's for a good cause," she said warmly. "And promise you'll let me come over and help first thing tomorrow."

"I promise," Enid said happily. "Thanks again for the party, Liz."

Elizabeth grinned. She could tell Enid had only one thought on her mind, and that was getting home to start preparing in earnest for her grandmother's arrival!

Does Enid realize how much her life will change when her grandmother moves in? Find out in Sweet Valley High #43, HARD CHOICES.